REACHER

REACHER

THE STORIES BEHIND THE STORIES

FEATURING A NEW, ORIGINAL REACHER SHORT STORY
"A BETTER PLACE"

LEE CHILD

THE MYSTERIOUS PRESS
NEW YORK

REACHER

Mysterious Press
An Imprint of Penzler Publishers
58 Warren Street
New York, N.Y. 10007

Copyright © 2025 by Lee Child

Quote on pg. 4 from "Born Under a Bad Sign"
by Albert King (lyrics by William Bell).

Quote on pg. 185 from "Blue Moon" by
Richard Rodgers and Lorenz Hart.

First edition

Interior design by Maria Fernandez

All rights reserved. No part of this book may be reproduced in whole or in part without written permission from the publisher, except by reviewers who may quote brief excerpts in connection with a review in a newspaper, magazine, or electronic publication; nor may any part of this book be reproduced, stored in a retrieval system, or transmitted in any form or by any means electronic, mechanical, photocopying, recording, or other, or used to train generative artificial intelligence (AI) technologies, without written permission from the publisher.

Library of Congress Control Number: 2025935474

ISBN: 978-1-61316-706-9
eBook ISBN: 978-1-61316-707-6

10 9 8 7 6 5 4 3 2 1

Printed in the United States of America

CONTENTS

Introduction *by Lee Child*   ix

ESSAYS

Killing Floor (1997)	1
Die Trying (1998)	7
Tripwire (1999)	13
Running Blind (2000)	21
Echo Burning (2001)	27
Without Fail (2002)	33
Persuader (2003)	39
The Enemy (2004)	45
One Shot (2005)	51
The Hard Way (2006)	59
Bad Luck and Trouble (2007)	65
Nothing To Lose (2008)	71

Gone Tomorrow (2009)	79
61 Hours (2010)	87
Worth Dying For (2010)	95
The Affair (2011)	101
A Wanted Man (2012)	109
Never Go Back (2013)	119
Personal (2014)	129
Make Me (2015)	139
Night School (2014)	151
The Midnight Line (2017)	163
Past Tense (2018)	173
Blue Moon (2019)	183

NEW REACHER SHORT STORY

A Better Place	191
Afterword *by Otto Penzler*	217

INTRODUCTION

I was first published in 1997, nearly thirty years ago as of this writing, in an era that now feels as remote as the Jurassic in the book business. The world was still almost entirely pre-internet. I had heard of email, vaguely, but I didn't have it. Nor did anyone else I knew. My first editor's comments arrived by fax, to an obliging local store, because I didn't have a fax machine either. I communicated with my agent by letter or landline telephone. I delivered my manuscripts as bulky packages in the mail.

The upside of that era was that brick-and-mortar bookstores had not yet been laid to waste. In fact they were thriving. New York had four excellent crime-fiction stores, and most cities had at least one or two. Their proprietors loved the genre and knew it intimately. They would call each other or get together at genre conventions to talk about hot new books and authors.

That's how I got my start. Those so-called "big mouths" talked up *Killing Floor* and turned it into a major release within the genre. It became a cult hit within the community. It won several Best First Novel prizes. I had arrived at the starting line.

Naturally (and of course quite rightly) by the time my second book came out, those folks had moved on to even-newer books and writers. All except one. The only "big mouth" who talked up *Die Trying* was a guy named Otto Penzler. He owned The Mysterious Bookshop in Midtown Manhattan, and was a voice worth having on your side. He was a world-renowned collector and a world-renowned Sherlock Holmes expert. He pushed *Die Trying* just as hard as anyone had pushed *Killing Floor*. I was grateful for that.

Otto also ran his own indie publishing company, The Mysterious Press, and was the editor of countless short-story anthologies and other ventures. He had more pies than fingers. He was always doing

INTRODUCTION

something, including beautifully bound special editions of titles likely to appeal to his customer base. Slowly, over the years, we became good friends, despite his irascible nature and appalling politics. On the plus side, he was a Yankees fan who had seen Mickey Mantle in his prime, he often had appealing wives or girlfriends, he had immaculate taste in food and champagne, he was funny in the kind of sardonic way that appealed to the Brit in me, and he was a gentleman. We got along very well.

Eventually he asked if he could do specially bound editions of the Reacher series. I had been asked once or twice before by other people, and I had always resisted the notion. Many of my readers were so into Reacher they felt they had to have every edition of everything. I didn't want them to feel obliged to shell out maybe a hundred bucks for a reprint of something they already had, but in a fancier jacket. So I had said no to such requests.

But Otto's special editions were also *limited* editions, only a hundred or so copies per title. His customer base was so big—and so rich—he could easily find a hundred people who really wanted the product and wouldn't even notice the price. So I felt there was no real risk of exploitation of the regular consumer. So I said yes.

Then he asked if I would write a foreword for each title, to add value and make each edition even more special. I wasn't sure how to respond. Certainly I was flattered that anyone would want to make or buy such handsome editions of my work, but felt quite unequal to providing literary insight into it, beyond what could be gleaned from, you know, actually reading it. I work with no plan, no theory, no structured approach, and no overarching intentions. I supposed I could pretend I had those things, and by using a little reverse engineering I could have come up with plausible explanations for why the books turned out the way they did. But the truth is I was always just hoping for the best, trusting my instincts, and flying by the seat of my pants.

So, self-indulgently, I decided to use the opportunity to do what I wish more authors would do: to set down a plain and quotidian record of the who, why, what, where, and when, like a career diary. I am not vain enough to think it important, or even very interesting; but—as a reader, pedant, and geek—I would like to know this kind of stuff about other authors' work, and therefore, humans being not so very different from one another, I assumed some readers, at least, might like to know this kind of stuff about mine. At worst, far in the future, if my daughter ever wanted to know where her dad was, and when, and what he was doing, and what he was thinking, she would have a shelf of handsome volumes to tell her exactly that.

—Lee Child
Cumbria, 2025

KILLING FLOOR

On Thursday, August 18th, 1994, in Manchester, England, I was told by senior management at Granada Television that my studio director's job was scheduled for elimination in an ongoing restructuring initiative and that, after a little more than seventeen years' service, I would be unemployed by Christmas. I didn't believe them. Given their competence level, I guessed early summer 1995 was a more likely exit date. (And I was proved right. I was eventually let go on June 21, 1995.)

I felt that British TV was in a death spiral—partly because people like them were in charge—and in any case employment elsewhere in the industry was unlikely. But I wanted to stay broadly in the world of entertainment, so I decided to act on a contingency plan I had thought of some years previously: I would write a novel.

So, to preempt the coming crisis, on Friday, September 2nd, 1994, I went to a stationery chain in the Arndale Centre, Manchester, and bought three pads of paper, a pencil, a pencil sharpener, and an eraser. I took them home, which was then in Kirkby Lonsdale, Cumbria, England, more than seventy miles away.

On Monday, September 5th, 1994, at home, at the dining room table, I sat down to write. An hour later, I gave the first chapter to my wife. I asked, "Should I continue?"

"Yes," she said. "I like it."

So I wrote through the rest of the fall and winter, at home and at work, and by March 1995 I had finished the book. But it wasn't this book. Not exactly. The working title was *Bad Luck and Trouble* (a title I re-used much later in the series) and the story was about drug money. A year or so earlier I had bought a book about money laundering—purely for its cover: it had a real dollar bill laminated into it. It said the illegal narcotics trade in the US was all cash (obviously), and in a dry, statistical way said its annual value was twice the amount of all the cash in circulation within the fifty states. Which, I saw, meant the cartels had a serious, industrial problem. I worked out that four thousand tons of paper money had to be transported to the Caribbean banks—twice a year.

The original manuscript was based around that theme.

I typed it up on my daughter's new laptop, and printed it out on her slow inkjet printer, and bought a copy of *The Writer's Handbook*, which lists agents, and I sent a query letter and the first three chapters to Darley Anderson, in London, England. He replied immediately, by letter (this was 1995, remember), and offered representation—and eventually, after seeing the whole draft, some editorial suggestions.

The suggestions were mostly to do with the story, but one was to change the title. Darley felt that the two negative words "Bad" and "Trouble" would trap readers' perceptions in the narrow niche of noir, which wouldn't help when seeking a wider, more generalist audience. So I came up with "Killing Floor" as an alternative, and it stuck. (The image of a meatpacking plant's killing floor was present in the text, and so were lines from the song "Born Under a Bad Sign"—including the line "Bad luck and trouble's been my only friend," which are still there, of course, as trace evidence of the working title.)

I worked on the suggestions and had the second draft completed by May 1995. Darley and I went through it again, and perfected a third draft by July. Nothing much happens in the world of publishing in August, so it was September 1995 before the book went out on submission. By that point I had been out of work for more than two months, and my savings were dwindling.

It was a targeted submission. Darley's movie co-agent knew an editor at Putnam in New York who was looking for that kind of thing: David Highfill. David liked the book and wanted to buy it.

But: he wanted me to change the story. He felt that drug gangs and drug money were overdone and overfamiliar. He wanted a major launch and major attention and felt that any element of same-old-same-old would blunt the impact.

I wanted—needed, I felt—to preserve the "river of money" theme. And I got lucky, because out in the real world, 1995 was the year the US had its first change in printed money for many decades. The $100 bill had been redesigned, and the new bill was being fed into circulation. There was tremendous journalistic coverage of the change, which was a move in the battle against counterfeiting. Some coverage was superficial, and some was very comprehensive. By reading it all, I saw how I could preserve the skeleton of the book by changing the flesh from narcotics proceeds to raw material for a counterfeiting operation.

I rewrote the book through the fall—over a year after starting it—and David liked what he saw, and on Thursday, December 7th, 1995, he made a formal two-book offer. At that point I was seven weeks away from going broke. I had enough in the bank for one more mortgage payment, but not two.

Putnam saw it as an early spring book—March, ideally—but March 1996 was too soon for them. Line editing, copy editing, jacket design, and preliminary marketing plans had to be done. So the book was scheduled for March 1997.

And eventually it was published in that month, on Tuesday, March 17th, Saint Patrick's Day. It had a truly great jacket image by Thomas Tafuri, a bloody handprint on a white background, and an author photograph taken by my then-sixteen-year-old daughter, of me sitting at the same table at which I had written the first pencil draft.

The book became an absolute exemplar of how things used to work: the specialist mystery bookstores and the crime fiction community adopted it as a favorite; it won every genre award it was eligible for; and without selling more than a respectable number it gave me a very solid start. Since then it has sold untold millions in, as of this writing, fifty languages and ninety-six countries.

I sold the dining table when we sold the house before our move to the States, but I still have the pencil. It sits on two pegs on a bulletin board in my office, and it reminds me every day of how this whole thing started.

DIE TRYING

My first book, *Killing Floor*, was substantially put to bed by the middle of March 1996, and slated for a publication date a year later. I realized—obviously—that if I wanted to publish a book a year, then I would have to write a book a year, which meant I should spend that pre-publication year writing the second book. Accordingly I started thinking about what became *Die Trying* at the beginning of April 1996.

At the time I was very interested in the separatist and militia movements in America, of which many still existed then, particularly in the Northwest. I saw them as fitting very clearly into the paranoid tradition of American politics, as ably described by Richard

Hofstadter. In particular I was fascinated by their self-serving mental gymnastics: total absence of evidence for wild fantasies was claimed to be definitive proof of their existence because only perfect government conspiracies could produce perfect cover-ups. I read extensively into the subject, and then did something I have never done since—I decided to make a research trip.

I was still living in the UK then, so I flew to Chicago and fitted in a short visit with my sister-in-law. I had been to Chicago several times before but for some reason on that occasion I noticed the huge number of dry cleaners in the area. *Chicagoans are very meticulous*, I thought, and later a dry cleaner showed up in the opening of the book.

Then I flew onward to Seattle and rented a car (a gray Ford Explorer, if you care) and drove back east, through the Washington State badlands, across the Idaho panhandle, and into Montana, as far as Kalispell and Whitefish. I had been paid for *Killing Floor* but was still some way from repairing my unemployed-broke-guy financial profile, and I had no credit cards, so it was cash all the way, including the planes and the car rental. (That was still possible—even somewhat normal—in 1996.) I stayed in twenty-dollar motels and ate cheap. I used truck stops and played pool in bars. I talked to all kinds of people—truckers, strippers, cops, farmers, FBI agents—and found my way into two separate militia encampments. I saw bears and coyotes and two-mile-long freight trains, and never quite got used to the vast emptiness, which at times was scary. At one point I drove four hours without seeing another vehicle.

But in the end it turned out to be more of a vacation than a research trip. I didn't really learn anything. The reality turned out to be more or less exactly what I had imagined. So I hustled back to Sea-Tac and flew home and started writing. I made rapid progress. I was full of energy and ideas.

The book's working title was *They the People*, to reflect the separatist angle. I started out with pencil and paper (as I had written all of *Killing Floor*) even though by then I had bought a basic Compaq laptop (in New York, with cash). I was worried that typing directly into the word processor (Windows Write, the 3.1 freebie, an excellent program for a novelist, I still think) would change the voice. But I tried it, and it didn't, so I carried on straight into the computer, which saved a lot of final-draft time.

The book's overall shape and approach were based on an instinctive decision to make it as fundamentally different as possible from *Killing Floor* while at the same time keeping it clearly part of a coherent series. I felt that authors could become as stereotyped as actors, and that if I did two similar books in a row I might get locked into a narrower channel than I wanted. I felt that if I used *Killing Floor* as a kind of "left field," and the new work as a kind of "right field," then I would be staking out a wide territory in between, in which I could roam free forever.

Accordingly, where *Killing Floor* was a one-track first-person narrative set in a small no-account rural town, I decided the new book should be a third-person, multiple-POV story involving glossy elements like the White House and the Hoover Building and the unlimited power of the state—which in particular seemed like an apt counterpoint to the bad guys' perspective. With that plan in mind, I maintained good progress—not least because a pre-published author has absolutely nothing else to do but write.

Only two things intervened, one ongoing, and one short and sharp. The short and sharp was a meeting with the UK publisher Transworld, on May 22nd, 1996 (my father's 72nd birthday, which is why I remember the date). I dropped in for a visit on the drive back from London. Transworld made a two-book offer a week later—May 29th, 1996—for *Killing Floor* and the work in progress, and has been my UK publisher ever since. After that—but not requiring involvement from me—my agent's foreign rights department quickly rolled up Holland, Germany, and Japan, in the first of what, as of this writing, totals ninety-seven territories worldwide.

The ongoing interruption was endless discussion with Putnam in the US about the title *Killing Floor*. There was concern (shared to some degree by Transworld) that a book with "killing" in the title wouldn't appeal to women readers, who might otherwise be interested in Jack Reacher. (Interestingly, that concern was recently echoed by my movie people, who love the first book but who, they say, *absolutely could not* title a movie *Killing Floor*. No, I don't know why, either.)

Accordingly, a lot of fruitless time was spent searching for alternatives. I still have doodled lists somewhere with dozens of increasingly desperate suggestions. But—as you know—in the end we stuck with *Killing Floor*, to no obvious commercial detriment.

And then . . . Putnam wasn't crazy about *They the People*, either. Did I have an alternative? Purely as a joke about the recent painful process, I said *Die Trying* . . . as in, we'll find something better, or die trying. But, "Great title!" they said, and it stuck.

I finished the book in December 1996, and it was quickly approved and accepted—still three months ahead of the first book's first publication. I remember feeling good about having the second book in the can so early, while simultaneously feeling worried that I had two books completed before I had received the first iota of reader feedback. It felt like a real gamble—but what else could a poor boy do?

TRIPWIRE

In the fall of 1996, my first book, *Killing Floor*, was still six months from publication, and I had almost finished my second, *Die Trying*. The various signature and delivery payments from a growing number of contracts had started to repair my unemployed-broke-guy status—I had a furnished office by that point, and my daughter, then sixteen and a big movie fan, felt the time was right to suggest a vacation in Orlando, Florida, so she could visit the Universal Studios theme park. In time-honored parental fashion, we negotiated—we would all go to Universal first, and then Key West afterward. Which we did, late in October.

Then when I got back I finished *Die Trying* and sent it in—physically, by courier, in those days. (Which was a significant expense for a newbie author living in the UK with a publisher in New York but, happily, I found a way of getting my manuscripts there for free. At the time the British Post Office ran a guaranteed overnight service—to compete with FedEx and UPS, I suppose—but possibly because I didn't live in a major city, or possibly because it was British, it never took less than two days to deliver a package, so it refunded my money every time, under its guarantee.)

I went on vacation again, in January 1997, to the Caribbean, and I remember getting a fax at the hotel from my editor at Putnam, formally accepting *Die Trying*. (I didn't have email until over a year later. Not that I was ever an early adopter. I didn't even have my own fax machine. All the edits for *Killing Floor* and *Die Trying* came via fax from New York to a bookstore near where I lived. Bruce, the owner, would call me and I would drop in and pick up the latest. He also sold me a *Webster's Dictionary*, which I still use.)

After that second vacation I had about six weeks before the US launch of *Killing Floor* and I used them to start my third book, *Tripwire*, which at that point I was calling *The Hook*. Strictly speaking I was writing it on spec—I had no contract for anything beyond *Die Trying*. But whereas publishers are always gloomy (like farmers, no year is ever a good year, and next year will probably be worse), this was still early 1997 and the industry was nothing like it is now, so I saw no real reason to anticipate insecurity. I set to work with a will and had finished the first three chapters by early March.

The initial idea had come from things I had read about Vietnam MIAs, the careful exhumation of remains, and their transportation to the identification lab in Hawaii. The process was quite rightly respectful—almost reverential—but I felt it spoke to a kind of collective trauma. Sadly, twentieth-century wars produced countless MIAs—technically KIA/BNR, killed in action, body not recovered—but the two thousand or so from Vietnam loomed large, possibly because it was a war with a confusing genesis and an unsatisfactory outcome. (By contrast, World War One produced an average of two thousand KIA/BNR *every single day*. But we won.)

Added to which I was full of ideas for characters and sub-plots, and indeed I look back on this book as having been the easiest and most joyful of all to write. It almost wrote itself. (Thinking about the books for these essays makes me realize how full of energy and ideas I was back then. Not that the tank is empty now—but the pressure in the fuel line is lower than it was.)

I set Reacher's early scenes in Key West because I had enjoyed the place the fall before (and because doing so would make the vacation retrospectively tax deductible). I set the early New York City scenes inside the World Trade Center in lower Manhattan. I love New York City's epic buildings—and as a writer I was interested in what goes on inside them, which often isn't really epic at all. The Empire State Building, for instance, is a glamorous icon on the outside, but on the inside, on its business floors, it's a shabby warren of tiny, plain, outdated office suites, leased by various desperate, failing, marginal, and sometimes shady operations.

The World Trade Center was the same. It was less outdated because it was built forty years later, it had a great lobby at street level, and a famous restaurant on the top floor but, in between, those towers were workaday places. Some big banks had leased swanky floors but most tenants were small beer, just scufflers and chancers working the angles, like Hook Hobie in this book. At the time, that's why I chose those buildings—I wanted to explore the difference between the iconic exterior and the grubby interior. But then, of course, four and a half years later, the World Trade Center became a symbol for something else entirely.

But that was all still ahead. In the story I got Reacher as far as New York City and then I headed there in reality for the launch of *Killing Floor*. Putnam did not fund the visit—it was a debut novel with no existing fan base—but a transatlantic coach fare wasn't ruinous, and I could afford a couple of nights in a cheap hotel. The first harbinger came at the departure gate, where I was upgraded to business class, and the good feeling continued. In galleys *Killing Floor* had gotten attention from genre stores, and clearly it was set to be a perfect example of how things used to work. Word-of-mouth in the genre community was going to give me a solid start. I met booksellers, signed stock, and above all had the thrill of seeing the book on the shelves.

I ran out of hotel money, so for the second half of the trip I stayed with my in-laws an hour outside the city. I got in and out by train. (Which is how I know I left for the trip after writing Chapter Three—all the commuter train stuff in Chapter Four was fresh in my mind when I got back. And I remember late one night at my in-laws I caught *A Few Good Men* on TV, with Tom Cruise, who I would work with fourteen years later on the *Jack Reacher* movie, with my daughter, by then thirty-one and still a movie fan, acting as my "people" so effectively that the producers bought a TV pilot from her. Little did I know.)

Then I flew home and wrote, and wrote, and finished *The Hook* by December 1997 for publication in the spring of 1999, thereby establishing a pattern of staying more than a year ahead. I had gotten a second deal, for books three and four, just after the Frankfurt Book Fair in the fall—enhanced, again, by a piece of good luck. My publisher had seen a rival reading *Killing Floor* and wanted to quash the competition.

But Putnam maintained its tradition of worrying about titles. I felt *The Hook* caught what I wanted to catch—a reference to the villain, of course, but also to his business model, his methods of entrapment, and to the whole idea of suspense storytelling, I thought. The reader has to swallow the hook. But very late in the game I got a call from New York saying people felt *The Hook* had a taste of *Peter Pan* about it—with Captain Hook. I wasn't convinced, but I was new, and at the time Putnam was run by one of the titans of the industry. My editor suggested *Tripwire*, which I felt was bland and somewhat lazy—as if he had started reading and then stopped at the first interesting word. But he was immoveable. And so *Tripwire* it became.

It was duly published in 1999 and it built on the first two books' sales, solidly but not spectacularly. Back then a series didn't have to be instantly massive. I look back on it with great affection, and more than a little nostalgia, for a number of reasons. As I said, it was a joy to write; it was the last book I wrote without all the hoopla that began to intrude a year or so later and, I suppose, because back then the Twin Towers were just another location. I can't think about the book without feeling, yes, I remember, that was back when I was the new kid on the block, and when New York City was what it used to be.

Both the blink of an eye, and a long time ago.

RUNNING BLIND

Running Blind was written in 1998, which was a big year for me. My daughter Ruth was due to finish high school in July, and we had decided to move from the UK to the US that summer. I started to write in February, while my wife Jane was away house-hunting. She found a place an hour north of New York City, and we put our own house on the market. We didn't want to take much with us—just books, paintings, CDs, and clothes, really—so we developed a fantasy in which a returning ex-pat couple would buy the house with all its contents.

And that's exactly what happened. It was the first of many magic moments that year. The buyers weren't exactly returning ex-pats—they were retired people who had just divorced their respective spouses and gotten married. Both divorces had been amicable in the sense that they had left their old homes intact and planned to start anew. They bought all our furniture, all our pots and pans, all our cups and saucers, all the silverware. The lawyers had advised a full inventory, so one day the buyers came over and we listed everything. I remember being in the kitchen, counting plates and so on. We opened a cupboard and said, "Oh, that's just olive oil and soy sauce and stuff like that . . . we'll clear it out before we go." "No," they said, "leave it—we need that stuff."

I continued writing whenever I could, amid all the form-filling and booking and faxes and signing. The story I had in mind was a blend of a classic locked-room mystery and a serial killer novel. With a twist at the end. The victims all were going to be female, but I didn't want to make it gratuitously gruesome, so I made the MO both intriguing (I hoped) and notably antiseptic—with no sign of a break-in or a struggle, the victims were being drowned in bathtubs of camouflage green army paint. How? Why? By whom? As always I wrote no outline and made no plan, and just figured it out as I went along. The subplot, or sub-text, or whatever an English major would call it, was going to be the relationship between Reacher and Jodie. I felt that the realities of their respective natures would gradually intrude on the euphoria of their re-encounter in the previous book, *Tripwire*. Reacher's eternal problem is that the kind of woman he falls for can't put up with him, in a kind of romantic catch-22.

As I said, it was a happy year, with a lot of excitement and many moments of magic. I had dreamed of living in New York literally since the age of four. My wife was itching to go home, and my daughter was looking forward to Wesleyan University, where she had gotten early acceptance. The mood was very positive, and therefore it interested me that Reacher turned out to be at his most irascible and impatient throughout the book. I was in a great mood, and he wasn't. In subsequent years I also found the opposite to be true. Some kind of internal auto-compensation mechanism, maybe, and one for the theorists.

The last line I wrote in the UK was in Chapter 14, during a scene in which Jodie begins to express unease about Reacher's attitudes. He has engineered a local gangster's demise:

"And I told you not to do that," she said.

Then we left the country.

We went by ocean liner for two reasons: we had a dog, and we didn't want to put her in an airplane hold, and because insurance on container consignments was compulsory, expensive, and pro-rata with the value of the contents. The ocean liner allowed unlimited baggage—even a car, if you wanted to take one—so we bought trunks and hand-carried the most expensive stuff, thereby lowering the container insurance to the point where the saving more or less paid for the liner tickets. And it was a perfect emigration-immigration experience—very reminiscent of history, very relaxing, and a very well-defined transition between old and new. We watched England disappear behind the stern, and then five days later we saw the Statue of Liberty approaching through the morning mist.

A day later I left on promotion tour for my second book, *Die Trying*.

It was my first real tour. No writer tours for his first book—there's no point: no audience yet, no name recognition. It's different for the second book—but not very different. Crowds were small, and events were intimate. But I loved every minute. I saw places I hadn't been before and realized the lovely truth of book touring: no one shows up who doesn't already like you. It's a warm bath. I got home (more accurately to the place that was going to be home) and carried on writing, stopping every evening in time for the first pitch in what was an amazing baseball season—for the '98 Yankees in particular, and for the sport in general.

The book was finished by the time the leaves in our new yard were turning golden, and then started the annual title hassle. My working title had been *The Visitor*, which I felt was both benign (what's nicer than a visitor arriving at the door?) and therefore, because of the genre implication, obviously sinister, too, but Putnam, with a familiar (from the previous year) but weirdly attuned sensibility, thought *The Visitor* was too sci-fi. "Browsers will think of visitors from outer space," the marketers said. I didn't agree, but I was still new, so I caved. Putnam titled the book *Running Blind*, which I privately called *Running Bland*.

My UK publishers didn't cave. They were still exasperated by the previous year's change, from *The Hook* to *Tripwire*, which they felt was very much for the worse, and went ahead with *The Visitor*. Which was a huge mistake on my part. I should have mandated uniformity, for better or worse. In 1998 publishers were not yet aware deep down of the internet's influence, and weren't thinking instinctively about international travel. I lost count of complaints from readers who bought the book online, or in foreign airports, thinking it was a story they hadn't yet read, and being disappointed, and blaming me for deceptive profiteering. During the year I made up my mind I would henceforth choose my own titles, come what may.

For what it's worth (not much, really, because the markets are very different), *The Visitor* did better pro-rata in the UK than *Running Blind* did in the US, despite a low-price experiment in America, possibly because of deep pink cover art in England (a color that experience has taught me often does well). But in both places it was solidly incremental, showing the kind of progress publishers used to be happy with. I felt my new career was establishing well, and I sat down to write the next in the series. But more about that in the next volume.

ECHO BURNING

Echo Burning was the fifth in the Jack Reacher series, the first to be written entirely inside the United States, and the first to be published without a squabble over the title. I started it in January 1999, about five months before the third installment, *Tripwire*, was due to be published, hence keeping up with my early decision to stay well ahead. Which was easier in those days. The promotion effort behind *Die Trying* in July 1998 had been relatively extensive—more than three weeks on the road, as I recall—and *Tripwire* was slated to receive similar treatment, but between those annual marathons I had absolutely nothing to do except write. Email was still in its infancy (for me anyway), and I had no cell phone at that time. Not that anyone would have written or called in any event. I had just two books on the market, one still in hardcover, and while warmly supported by the genre community, in a wider sense obscurity would have been a giant leap forward. I remember feeling that if I kept on working hard, kept on showing up once a year, one foot in front of the other, then something might happen eventually. In retrospect I much prefer where I am now to where I was then, but the memory of all those uninterrupted days is still faintly golden. We were living in a house in Pound Ridge, New York, and my office was a spare bedroom that looked out over a pond. Life was good.

As always the book was written without a plan or an outline, except for three things that had stuck in my mind. The first was the Ben Franklin quote: "Three people can keep a secret if two of them are dead." I knew I wanted to build the plot reveals around that proposition. The second was a trip I had taken through west Texas the previous summer. There had been an annual sequence of ferocious heat waves in Texas (which would continue), with record numbers of consecutive days over a hundred degrees.

This was literally a new world for a guy from Britain, where a day that peaks over seventy is routinely referred to as a "scorcher." The physical impact was fascinating. As was the emptiness. The US Census Bureau calls anywhere with fewer than five or six people per square mile "uninhabited," and by that measure a lot of west Texas was indeed uninhabited. The isolation was fantastic. I met a woman who told me if she wanted to eat something she didn't kill or grow herself, she had to drive five hours to the nearest store—and five hours back. So I knew the book would have a hot, empty feel.

The third thing on my mind was to try to keep readers unsure about the main female lead. Is she good or bad? Telling the truth or lying? That would be important for the mystery element of the story, but it would be a challenge. I couldn't afford for her to be unlikable. But I set to work cheerfully, with great energy, with nothing but plenty of time ahead.

The manuscript survived an early technological scare. My trusty Compaq laptop blew up—but quietly, so I didn't notice immediately. The power supply failed, so the battery was no longer charging, and it was well into the red zone before a warning popped up. I'm a competent electrician (and a qualified firefighter, too, both legacies of my theater tech days), albeit somewhat previous-generation when it comes to modern stuff, but I theorized that the wall voltage might go to a separate transformer winding than a twelve-volt input, so I carried the dying computer out to my car and plugged it into the cigarette lighter, and I got enough juice to rescue the data to a floppy disk. (Remember them?) Then I drove to a store and bought a new computer, easing into the realization that computers were going to be items with short and transitory life spans, rather than the consumer durables I thought they were. (Remember consumer durables?)

I worked on patiently, and took a long break for the launch of *Tripwire*, for which I was on the road in the UK for a week or so, and then in the US for twenty-eight days. That book did well in both countries, in an incremental, under-the-radar way, which in a sense made me feel good, and in another sense made me understand (yet again) what an immense task it is to penetrate the culture deeply enough to become an automatic seller, or a household name. But there seemed to be time, so *patience* was very much the watchword that year. I got home and continued working, and the sun shone, and the Yankees kept winning, and all was good.

My working title all along was *Echo Burning*, which two words I liked for their sound, and *Burning* seemed to work for the heat, and the brewing tensions in the story, and *Echo* seemed convincing as a name for a county in that vast, empty part of the world. And after four consecutive wrangles over titles I was determined that it would stick, and it did, even though neither English-language publisher really liked it. But I was no longer new, and in the gentler world of the late 1990s I was seen as an established prospect about halfway through his break-in phase, so they let me have my way. The book was published in the early summer of 2001, and I look back on it now as a solid piece of work, with plenty of spinning plates, decent pace, and good intrigue. But I suppose what impresses me most was its (or my) evident appetite for a long, dense, complicated story, the contemplation of which would now cause a mild panic: how could I keep track of it all, when there's so much else to do every day? But as I said, those were simpler times, with nothing else to do all day except dream stuff up, and then write it.

WITHOUT FAIL

Without Fail was the sixth story in the Jack Reacher series, and it had an interesting publication history. It debuted in early summer 2002 but it was completed well before that, as was my habit and luxury in those days. The fourth book in the series, *Running Blind*, came out in the early summer of 2000, with the fifth, *Echo Burning*, already delivered and awaiting its place in the pipeline. So I started *Without Fail* in September 2000 and worked through the winter into 2001, aiming to deliver it before *Echo Burning* was published, thereby maintaining my one-year grace period.

In terms of process I remember being about half done by Christmas and early in January our daughter—by then a junior in college—left for a semester overseas. In practical terms I don't see why it made a difference that she was studying in another country rather than another state, but somehow a calm and a focus descended on our household, and I wrote the second half of the book in just a few weeks in a rush of creativity that I wish visited more often. (For those interested in nicotine dependency—not many of you, I'm sure—the only negative was the constant torrent of triggers—a completed sentence, paragraph, page—that led me to smoke too much. In fact, as a result, during the second half of the book I changed to so-called light cigarettes and have stayed with them ever since.)

In terms of broad content, I knew I wanted to write about the Secret Service. I had struck up an occasional relationship with President Bill Clinton, who was—and remains—a voracious reader, unafraid of extensive excursions into our genre, and who had the habit of writing or calling the author of a book he had enjoyed. As a result I had gotten to know some of his protection agents, and they struck me as hugely competent individuals, backed up by virtually limitless resources and sophisticated techniques, yet quite naturally worried about the tiny wild card or X factor that could lead to absolute catastrophe and the most public failure imaginable. The constant tension between reasonable self-confidence and reasonable self-doubt seemed to define them. It was a theme I wanted to explore.

In narrower terms, as always, I tried to keep my eye on two factors: firstly, how to get a habitual loner like Reacher into the story without over-reliance on yet another creaky wrong-place-wrong-time coincidence; and how to give a habitual loner like Reacher a sense of emotional background, without dwelling too much on his feelings, which he simply wouldn't do. I decided on a two-birds-with-one-stone solution, in that I would have Reacher's dead brother's ex-girlfriend initiate contact, for professional reasons only, which got him into the action quite plausibly, and which then allowed him to be affected both by memories of the sibling he had lost and by current-day feelings for the ex-girlfriend.

The ex-girlfriend was a Secret Service agent with the name M. E. Froelich, which came from the winner of a charity auction. There's an auction at each of our annual genre conventions, usually benefiting a literacy project in the locality, and an idea took hold in the late 1990s whereby instead of donating a signed first edition or other item of physical memorabilia, authors would offer the high bidder the chance to have his or her name in an upcoming book as a character. Accordingly I offered such a prize, and two women bid the lot up to dizzying heights, until I said both could be in the book. The other woman was Frances Neagley, then a nurse from San Francisco, now retired. Her character, Reacher's old colleague from his army days—shadowy, mysterious, unexplained—seemed to work so well I brought her back in two later installments, which ran counter to my general decision to avoid soap-opera structures, with their repertory casts of supporting characters.

Thus the book took shape over the winter, and I delivered it in March 2001, about fifteen months ahead of its slated publication slot in June 2002. Two things happened during those fifteen months. One was a private, inside-baseball issue; the other was public. The private issue was that the book, being my sixth, completed my third two-book contract with Putnam, and as had also happened at the end of the second contract, Random House lobbied me to join them. This time I listened. I am an instinctively loyal person, and Putnam had done a fine job; indeed, this is as good a place as any to place on record my sincere appreciation for everything they did. In particular my Putnam editor David Highfill deserves credit (or blame, I suppose) for being the single most significant influence (after the author) on the Reacher series as a whole, even today.

But doing a fine job doesn't preclude someone else doing a better job, and the evidence was mounting. The nuts and bolts of the thing seemed to favor the larger Random House, and the intangibles, which are of great importance day to day, seemed to favor Random House too. The nature of the intangibles renders a precise calculus impossible, so our advice to each other is always both cynical and naive: go where the love is.

I went to Random House, which meant *Without Fail* became what's called an "orphan book," which means a book that comes out after the publisher has lost its active interest in the author. Tradition demands that such a book should get no marketing, no promotion, no publicity, no attention at all, and that was this book's fate. It didn't sell too badly, even so.

The public event was, of course, 9/11, which, right down there at the bottom of the list, changed book reviews in 2002. *Without Fail*'s plot, while nothing remotely to do with Islamic terrorism, was seen as a White House-in-danger story, and therefore it got mentions, and the general wave of patriotism made good reviews of it mandatory. And the role of the author changed subtly, too. The relentless news cycles needed content, and opinions were sought in unlikely places, and gradually writers were assumed to be experts. On one occasion it happened to me, literally overnight. I went to Holland to launch *Without Fail*, and I got on the plane a fiction writer, and I got off a security expert, because a politician named Pim Fortuyn had been assassinated. All my TV spots and radio interviews were moved from showbiz to news. What should we have done differently? How could we have better protected him? What techniques should we know about? How can we learn?

What alarmed me was how happily I played the part.

PERSUADER

Persuader was the seventh Reacher story overall, but the first for the new publisher, which makes me remember it as something of a reboot of the series. Not that Reacher was ever just about brawn—for instance, in *Killing Floor*, the first book, one of the vital clues was the difference between the placement of the singular possessive apostrophe and the plural possessive—but I very much wanted to recapture the manic physicality of some of the earlier books. I had been very happy with *Without Fail*, the preceding installment, but couldn't escape the feeling it was a little calm, even cerebral. I decided to return to first-person narrative, which I hadn't used since *Killing Floor*, and to make the story a full-on bloodbath.

I had the title in mind, which comes from the name of a Mossberg shotgun—is there a sound more persuasive than the *crunch-crunch* of a pump action?—and I had ideas about a gang suspected of drug smuggling actually being involved in weapons smuggling instead, and I had picked out the gray coast of Maine in April as a location. And I wanted the opening sequence to be an homage to Alistair MacLean's trick at the start of *Fear is the Key*, from 1961. (I was and remain a MacLean fan, without being unaware of his value as a cautionary tale—the later laziness and alcoholism were both to be avoided, for instance—if possible.)

So, as always, I started writing on September 1st. September 1st, 2001, that is. Which meant I stopped again ten days later, on 9/11.

Now, no one is, or should be, even remotely, interested in the effect 9/11 had on me personally, or on my writing process. There are a million more important issues, and I happily, gratefully, and delightedly take my place at the absolute bottom of the list of those concerns. But these essays are supposed to record what I was doing and how I was thinking, so for that reason alone I will outline what threatened to become an existential impasse for me.

I had grown up in England, where widespread wartime bombing was part of the culture and of very recent memory, and where a constant trickle of terrorist activity was a given, through my teenage years and beyond. In the past, well-loved buildings had disappeared overnight, and innocent civilians had been killed in the tens of thousands, then thousands, then hundreds, and then they were being killed in the dozens, by different enemies. So I was less stunned by 9/11 than my neighbors. But possibly more outraged, because it hurt to see a fundamentally decent nation so violated.

But my problem was—and again, I gratefully concede my problems were entirely, completely, utterly trivial—I had been living with fiction literally my entire working life. Theater, television, and novels—I lived in a world of story, and in the fall of 2001, story didn't work.

Specifically, it didn't work for the New York Yankees. Imagine the outline proposal, or the elevator pitch: New York City is attacked by a shattering outrage, there's smoke and fire and grief, nothing could be worse, but the Yankees get to the World Series, and win, and New Yorkers walk a little taller the next day, and the healing begins.

That's what should have happened. Hollywood would buy that story. Every fiber of my fiction instincts told me that was how it would turn out.

But it didn't. The Yankees lost, after a Series of great drama. Games four and five were pure story: unbelievably unlikely wins. Game six was pure story: a one-night collapse, to set up the ninth-inning win in game seven.

But it was a ninth-inning loss in game seven.

Fiction had failed me. I was profoundly upset, in the literal meaning of the word. I didn't want to do it anymore. It was a meaningless waste of time. It meant nothing. It had no value.

Looking back, I suppose there was a measure of general shock involved in my reaction, and eventually I got back to work, but I missed my deadline—for the first and only time in my life—but because I was still a year ahead in those days it didn't really matter. I ended up happy with the book, and I was consoled, both personally and existentially, by the reaction. In great numbers, readers wrote in, saying basically, "I wish Jack Reacher was real, because we really need him in times like these." I realized story was still working for some and, like a man recovering from a broken leg, perhaps, I got my fiction mojo back.

In the interests of full disclosure, however, I must report I got my worst-ever review for this book: an online commenter wrote: "I hated this book. I'm sorry I read it. I wish I could un-read it." Which helped too, in a way. Normality was back, with all its snark and petty concerns.

THE ENEMY

The Enemy was my eighth book overall, the second for my new publisher, and because I was still a year ahead in terms of delivery, it was written after the sixth book, *Without Fail*, was launched, but well before the seventh, *Persuader*, came out. And given that comments on *Without Fail* were at that point too new to have an effect on the work-in-progress, if *The Enemy* betrays reader feedback, which I think it does, that feedback must have come from the first five books in the series.

Those first five books had not been bestsellers, but they had garnered a solid audience, which was beginning to organize itself into a hardcore online community. Members were starting to call themselves "Reacher Creatures," and their comments and questions were starting to flood my website message board. I was gratified to have such a passionate bunch of readers, and I felt lucky to be on the upswing in 2002, just as the internet was changing from geeky to normal.

Their comments and questions were many and various, but my overall sensation was one of watching the "ownership" of Reacher migrate outward, and his acceptance as a fixture in readers' imaginations, as a reality fit to be discussed and speculated about. There is no finer reward for an author, of course, and no more interesting process than eavesdropping on the conversation as a mute third-party bystander. Gradually a consensus question emerged among the readers: If *this* is what he's like *now*, what was he like when he was inside the big green machine?

I decided to answer that question by writing a prequel. Not an origin story as such; more properly a pre-prequel, I suppose, not the last step on the road but the next-to-last. Reacher in the army, mid-career, fully immersed.

Which gave me the chance to pick a year. Instead of writing in the vague present, I could choose a specific era. Reacher's fictional service ran from 1983 to 1997, between which years many interesting things happened. Mid-career would suggest about 1990, where we find the most interesting thing of all, at least to the military—the sudden collapse of Communism. The Berlin Wall was coming down. They had given up. We had won. The 1989-1990 holidays were happy indeed.

Or were they? Uniquely for the military, victory means defeat. If the enemy has disappeared, politicians will say we no longer need what disappeared it. I pictured a kind of dull shudder passing through the immense organization: What next?

In the real world, and in normal military fashion, the answer and the consequent shudder came not at the time, but a little later, which turned out to be about ten years before I started thinking about the book, which meant the events had been covered extensively by all kinds of recent-history journalism. The reaction was delayed because the fall of Communism had not been predicted. So for the purposes of fiction I compressed the timescale, to remove the delay, to make the pride in the past and the fear for the future simultaneous. The issue, of course, was tanks. There was tank terrain galore, where East met West. The conflict would start with history's biggest tank battle. Except it didn't. So the armored divisions, once kings of the world, were now yesterday's news. Maybe much smaller, much more agile units would be required. The future looked full of small wars. Helicopters, mostly. No need for a thousand tanks.

I felt it was a dramatic period. And it had another advantage: Reacher's family was still alive. His mother and his brother, at least. His brother, Joe, died at the start of events in the first book, *Killing Floor*, which was a necessary decision both for the plot, and more importantly to establish Reacher as completely alone in the world. The Mysterious Loner has to be alone. The character doesn't work otherwise. But I felt, and readers agreed, that Joe was somehow still a presence in the series. Reacher thought about him, and mentioned him from time to time, and he was a major figure in *Without Fail*, despite being dead six years by then. So I was very happy to get the chance to write him alive, walking and talking, with Reacher in the role of little brother for once, and both of them in the role of kids when they visit their mother.

The mother storyline was dictated by my chosen chronology, but I would have compressed the timescale anyway, for drama. I won't give away any plot spoilers, in case you haven't read the book yet, or don't remember it, but the "walking out of the movie" speech Reacher's mother delivers, and the dialogue before and after it, is some of the writing I'm happiest with. There was something important I wanted to tell my daughter, but some things are hard to say, so I had Reacher's mother tell Reacher and his brother instead. Many readers say they appreciate her sentiments. (But later in the book, I was equally happy with Reacher's soliloquy that starts: *What is the twentieth century's signature sound?* I thought that was a fine, fine paragraph, but no one ever mentions it.)

But obviously the main challenge—and the main enjoyment—would be writing Reacher not slightly older and wiser this time, as would be usual, but slightly younger and dumber. Eight years' worth of younger and dumber, technically. But still mid-career. Maybe at the peak of his powers, in a brisk, brash kind of a way. Thirty years old, a major, a go-to guy. Energetic, still loyal, his faith as yet unshattered. I started writing in the fall of 2002, with a man dying of a heart attack. I think I was feeling morbid. Hence the coded message to my daughter, I suppose. Then the body is found and Reacher gets the call. He's a working MP, pulling night duty on New Year's Eve, and the book is his first-person narrative, the second in a row after *Persuader*, which was unusual for me. First-person narratives are rarer than third-person in the series as a whole. But I felt the establishing pre-origin story should have first-person's intimacy.

I liked the book as I wrote it. I had plenty of ideas stacked up—too many, possibly—but I was happy to let the story go where it wanted. The big reveal about Reacher's mother's one-time employment was completely spontaneous.

I wrote through the winter and finished in February 2003. By the summer the book was in pre-production, by which time I regretted the heart attack at the start. My agent's girlfriend died—of a heart attack. They had been together for twenty-five years. I had enjoyed her company many times. She was like a den mother, not that a small and sedate circle of writers really needed one. Her name was Adele King, and the book is dedicated to her.

ONE SHOT

This is the ninth title in the Reacher series. It was started in the fall of 2003, finished in the spring of 2004, and published in the spring of 2005. It was written in my upstairs office in my then home in Pound Ridge, New York. The original working title, as I recall, was *First Cold Shot*, but as time passed it filtered through the sniper's unofficial credo of *one shot, one kill*, and became the simpler *One Shot*. Unusually I had a fairly clear picture in my mind of the story's spine, and I remember sitting down with great enthusiasm to begin.

But the beginning was a risk. Reacher himself didn't appear for a long, long time. Normally the rule of thumb with character-driven series fiction is to introduce the protagonist early—on page one, ideally. The returning reader needs a sense of comfort and familiarity, and the new reader needs to know who the book is about, and both needs are usually met simultaneously and without delay. But I needed to establish a fairly complex set-up before Reacher arrived on the scene—an apparently random sniper atrocity in a heartland city, meticulously planned and perfectly executed, followed immediately by the corresponding police investigation, again very thorough, which results in the capture of the suspect. Only then is Reacher's name even mentioned. "Get Jack Reacher for me," the suspect says. But it's still a long time before Reacher actually arrives . . . on a bus, of course.

Years later that opening structure was crucial to Hollywood's decision to use the book as the basis for their first Reacher movie. More on that later. But first—and anecdotally—the opening had another consequence for one particular reader. Part of my method of building suspense in the first chapter was to delay the shooting with a meticulous account of the unknown sniper's on-site preparations, including a full description of his chosen rifle, and his chosen ammunition. Snipers can be geeky, with definite preferences. My research library suggested that custom Lake City ammunition was favored—a proprietary .308 boat-tail bullet, with gunpowder from a second source, in a casing from a third. But most of my research books are old, so in a rare outbreak of conscientiousness I called Lake City to make sure the ammunition was still on the market—firearms mistakes are relentlessly exposed by certain sections of the readership. The folks at Lake City confirmed it was indeed still currently available, and were so tickled to know their product would be in a book that they sent me a box of the real thing as a gift.

In those days I liked to give out small souvenirs or mementos of each book, to long-time fans and supportive booksellers, so we took the powder out of the freebie Lake City rounds (and replaced it with crushed peanut shells) and had *Lee Child One Shot* engraved on the casings. Lake City's own initials (by happy coincidence mine too, LC) were stamped on the bottom of the casings, and overall I thought the engraved rounds, polished like jewelry, made charming if sinister gifts. One woman got one, but on the way home it got trapped and hidden in an inner seam in her purse. She thought she had lost it. Months later she got married and left for her honeymoon, carrying the same purse through airport security. The hidden sniper round showed up clearly on the X-ray, and the woman was detained. She explained the round was a harmless souvenir from a book launch, but to no avail . . . until, after an hour, a senior TSA officer arrived and said, "Oh yeah, I read that book. It was great." The woman made her plane, but only just.

Also in chapter one was a provincial TV anchor I named Ann Yanni, which was a personal in-joke based on the fact that my foreign editions showed some Cyrillic typefaces transliterate *Lee Child* in forms that look like *Ann Yanni*. The suspect James Barr came from the Great Barr railroad station, which was nearest to my childhood home. A one-star general, back from Reacher's past, was named Eileen Hutton, after my audiobook publisher. And so on and so forth, a writer having fun in an indulgent manner. The geographic setting was never specified—I had in mind parts of Cincinnati as the "look"—but I wanted a generic heartland feel, without getting hung up on specifics. I made the bad guys ex-gulag prisoners from the Soviet era. I called the local DA (and therefore his defense-lawyer daughter) Rodin, which was taken as an homage to Freddie Forsyth's *The Day of the Jackal*, which also involves a sniper, of course, as well as a character named Rodin. But that assumption is inaccurate—the name was a shortened version (an "Ellis Island version") of a Russian name taken from a Red Army tank commander I had read about while writing the previous book, *The Enemy*. I wanted some doubt in the reader's mind whether the long-ago respectable Russian immigrants were somehow connected to the present-day criminal Russians.

Eventually the book was finished, and I thought it came out solid, with plenty of intrigue, action, reversals, and twists. I was happy with it. It waited a year and came out in 2005, and got a full-on and very complimentary review from Janet Maslin in the daily *New York Times*—my first in that forum. For many years Maslin was the *Times'* movie reviewer, and as a result she's still read and respected in Hollywood, and her review sparked a minor four-day feeding frenzy there. Paramount—allied with Tom Cruise's production company—offered a sensational deal, which we took, and which led to six years of on-again, off-again development before cameras finally rolled, in September 2011.

They chose *One Shot* as the first movie partly because it was the book that grabbed their attention in the first place, but mostly because Reacher's long-delayed entrance gave them time to "explain" the character by third-party references and descriptions before he actually appeared. In other words, rather than show Reacher on the screen and then stop to explain him, they could get the necessary exposition out of the way first, and then have Reacher show up and get into the action immediately. They thought the structure was perfect for the first outing in what they hoped would become a long-running franchise.

The movie was a full-scale major studio production, but day-to-day it felt more like an independent project, made only because the core cast and staff were Reacher fans. I had an open invitation to the set, which I enjoyed. Film sets were nothing new to me—I had been on hundreds in my previous TV job—and I had fun. They asked me to take a tiny cameo part—as a desk sergeant returning Reacher's minimal possessions on his release after a night in jail. They felt a cop handing back Reacher's toothbrush would also be the book writer handing a notional baton to the movie actor—meaning upon meaning.

I first saw the finished movie (by then re-titled *Jack Reacher*) a few months before its theatrical release. I liked it. The casting of Tom Cruise was controversial, of course, because he's smaller than Reacher. But I was relaxed. All actors are smaller than Reacher. I felt the pace and flow of the story carried it past that theoretical objection.

But I prefer the book, and I hope you do, too.

THE HARD WAY

The Hard Way was written on the move. In April of 2004 we sold our house in the New York suburbs and bought an apartment on 22nd Street in Manhattan. No more yard, no more pool. The idea was to head to our place in the south of France when we needed that kind of thing. Thus the book flew transatlantic with me many times, JFK to Nice on Delta and back, on a memory stick.

I started it in New York, with two things in mind. Firstly, it was the tenth title, and my UK publisher had been with me from the start, doing tremendous work throughout, so as a minor acknowledgement of that anniversary I decided to send Reacher to the

UK for the final sequences. And secondly, it was on my mind that the start of the previous book, *One Shot*, had been a bit of a narrative risk in that Reacher wasn't even mentioned for many pages, and didn't actually appear for many more. It worked, I thought, but it flew in the face of series theory. I had a sense of having gotten away with it. So I was determined to start the new book with the two words "Jack Reacher," which I did:

"Jack Reacher ordered espresso, double, no peel, no cube, foam cup, no china, and before it arrived at his table he saw a man's life change forever."

As well as immediately nailing who the story was about (and, economically, starting to characterize him), I saw it as an homage to certain classic thriller openings, which in turn I saw as the same way that George Shearing, for instance, played the piano: *This chord and this key is where we're going to end up; now stick around and see how we get there.* What man? How did his life change? I believe people are hard-wired to want the answer to questions. That's my narrative method—ask or imply a question, and then answer it very slowly.

Having just moved to the city, I set the opening answers there, starting at a restaurant on Sixth

Avenue in the West Village where I had been taken for one of my first publishing lunches back in the day. I changed the restaurant to a coffee shop and let things develop from there with a self-indulgent tour of the places I loved—the Dakota apartment building, West Broadway, shopping at the weird stores on the Bowery. Some of the characters were ex-pat Brits, like me. Looking back, I remember the story unspooled fairly effortlessly. Typing it out took time, of course (I'm a terrible typist—two index fingers only, real hunt-and-peck), but mentally the pressure in the pipes was high and the content just happened by itself. Random influences inserted themselves. I saw a guy I knew, writer Steve Brewer, and his name became the NYPD detective's. I talked to my assistant Maggie Griffin on the phone, and she had a bad cold, so the love interest Lauren Pauling has a husky voice. And so on. I made Pauling fifty-plus—I was turning fifty myself that year, and I remember thinking, hey, you don't have to be in your thirties to have some fun.

The first technical challenge was to abandon technical accuracy about certain aspects of New York—mostly the traffic situation. Because I lived there, I found myself writing journeys literally from

West 72nd Street, say, to the West Village—and I remember re-reading those sequences and realizing they felt like MapQuest pages on acid. I figured most people in the world knew the general shape of Manhattan—long and thin, uptown, downtown, east, west—so I decided to simplify directions for the sake of not getting bogged down in one-way streets. Thus I have people coming down the West Side Highway and turning left onto Houston Street, for instance, which isn't actually possible, but which sketches the geography in the way I wanted. It's an example of getting things right by deliberately getting them wrong. If it really matters to the plot that a street is one-way, then by all means make the point. If not, don't. That was my approach.

The second challenge was the second half of the story, in which Reacher goes to England. Most of the time I'm a foreigner writing America as if I were a native. Now I had to be a native writing England like a foreigner. What would Reacher notice? What would stand out? What would intrigue him, surprise him, confuse him? It wasn't too difficult—I have always been equally aware of the charms and the absurdities of my home country, and I had been away plenty long enough to notice them as if with fresh eyes. Some were easy—renting a tiny Mini Cooper and driving on the wrong side, and so on, and London feels like many of the world's great cities. I had in mind the denouement should be set in Norfolk, which is the northern half of what is called East Anglia, a (relatively!) large bulge on the east coast, where the American bomber bases were in World War Two. It's a flat area, full of drained marshes, mostly farmland—the UK equivalent of the Plains, and (again relatively) remote and inaccessible.

The action continued to unspool. Characters came and went, and a minor theme emerged, of love and loyalty between pairs of sisters. I remember deciding to dedicate the book to my nieces Kate and Jess, my writer-brother Andrew's girls, who were eight and five at the time, and a terrific pair of allies for each other. I finished the book in France, in early spring 2005. I remember being alone in the house—my wife had gone to Holland to look at the tulips. I remember feeling there was another chapter or two to go, but suddenly realizing no, that's the end right there.

And I have to place on record that *The Hard Way* generated the only freebie I have so far ever gotten, in response to what could be seen as product placement: in Chapter 37 I describe Reacher kicking down a door, and my style mandates a prior paragraph predicting the mechanics of so doing, starting with a description of the heavy shoes he's wearing, which were, of course, the same shoes I was wearing that day—bench-made brogues by a company named Cheaney, of Northampton, England. I looked down and described them. I was not raised poor, exactly (penny-pinching, rather than penniless), but I was left aware of the huge cultural difference between plastic shoes and leather, and shoes are the only apparel item I remain sensitive about. Someone at Cheaney read the paean and contacted me to say the company was delighted, and would I like a free pair? I said yes, and they duly dispatched them. (I still have them.) The style was named Tenterden, which in a further random connection is the name of a town in the county of Kent, England, which is near where we much later bought a country house, and where I shopped for furniture for the new library. Table lamps, too. And the Cheaney web site still lists, on the Tenterden page, the boast: *As worn by Jack Reacher, in the Lee Child Novel* The Hard Way. *Fame at last!*

BAD LUCK AND TROUBLE

Unusually, I can remember exactly when and where I got the idea for *Bad Luck and Trouble*. June 21st, 2005, at about eight in the evening, during a bookstore event in Naperville, Illinois, near Chicago. I was approaching the end of a massive world tour for *One Shot*. I had been on the road since April 3rd, in the UK, Europe, Australia, New Zealand, and America, and I was due home on July 10th. Those were the days! Back then I still had plenty of energy and an appetite for travel. I did it all again in 2010, but since then I haven't toured much. The conventional wisdom is that an author tours now so he won't have to later. That's what I reminded myself during those endless days. Plus I remembered a line from a television commercial for the Smith Barney brokerage house. The thirty-second spot showed hands-on investment advisers poking around dirty and uncomfortable factories, hoping to spot opportunities. The tag line was, "This is how we earn it." I repeated that line to myself at every early start, every delayed flight, and every eighteen-hour day.

By June 21st I had done the *One Shot* talk about a hundred times, so once it got rolling I was pretty much on autopilot, so the front part of my brain would wander during the show. That night I remembered that day's date at the top of the tour schedule page. June 21st seemed to mean something. It's my niece Katharine's birthday—my brother Andrew's elder daughter, nine years old that day, now in college majoring in biochemistry—but I knew that already, and we had sent a card, so it wasn't that issue nagging at me. It wasn't my wife's birthday, or my daughter's. It wasn't my wedding anniversary. So what was it?

About halfway through the spiel I figured it out. June 21st, 2005, was exactly ten years to the day since my last official day of employment in my previous career. In other words, it was my tenth anniversary of getting fired. Immediately—while I continued talking—a whole bunch of memories flooded back. I felt very nostalgic all of a sudden, mostly about the people I had worked with. They had been good friends. We had all been fired at the same time. What had happened to them all? Where were they now? What were they doing? Were they happy?

And then—while I continued talking—I started to wonder how my choices would stack up against theirs. I felt pretty good about how things were going, but I wondered how it would feel to get together again and compare. Would my life look crazy to them? Would I feel like the smart guy or the dumb guy?

Thus by the end of that evening's Q&A I had a soup-to-nuts outline for my next book. Reacher's old MP unit would reform on an unofficial basis, and he would work once again with the folks who had been closer than family. He would scrutinize them, and they would scrutinize him, and his feelings and their reactions would be revealed. Along the way they would work an ad-hoc high-stakes case that would ease them all back into their old professional dynamic.

I felt like it was a sound basis for a book. I have never believed in the old advice to write what you know. No one really knows enough for a good thriller. But I believe in writing what you feel. Most parents have had a panicked moment in the mall, when they look up and their kid is gone. All kinds of dread emotions flood in instantaneously. Happily most parents then glance the other way and hey, there's the little guy, happy as can be. But if you remember that initial dread, you can mine it and expand it into a book about a child kidnap. Lasting days and days, or even weeks. And so on.

My little department in the world of television was of course a million miles away from an army unit. Or was it? In terms of feeling rather than knowing, it could be said to have had similarities. We were numerically small. We felt we were special. We were embattled. We were under constant professional stress. We relied on each other totally. We spent more hours together than with our real families. We were defiant. The department was named after its principal work location—the Central Control Room, abbreviated to CCR. We had our own slogan—"You don't f**k with CCR." I tried to import all those feelings into

Bad Luck and Trouble, including a slogan, remembered fondly and a little poignantly—"You don't mess with the Special Investigators." Even though someone patently had, because all the special investigators were out of work. Like all of CCR was.

As I wrote, I felt the emotional foundation was working. I felt there was a genuine sense of reunion. I started in September 2005, initially in my new apartment on 22nd Street in Manhattan but mostly at my house in the south of France. My method is painfully linear. I can't go back and fill things in later. Hence the book was stuck at eleven words long for a day or two: "The man was called Calvin Franz and the helicopter was a . . ." because I needed to know what the helicopter was before I could continue. I walked down to the bookstore and bought a book about civilian rotary-wing aircraft. (Plus a lot of other interesting stuff that delayed me for a time.) Eventually I decided the helicopter was a Bell 222. Seemed plausible. So I wrote it down and continued. At that point I had no title. Later I thought of calling it *Little Wing*—a particularly lovely Jimi Hendrix song, and the name I gave to the fictional new missile system at the core of the story. But publishers felt no Reacher story could have "little" in the title. So I recycled *Bad Luck and Trouble*—a line from the old blues song "Born Under a Bad Sign" and the rejected working title from my first book, which was called *Killing Floor* instead. (Another blues song.) I felt *Bad Luck and Trouble* matched the mood of the new book pretty well.

The book was finished by March 2006, fourteen months ahead of its US publication in May 2007. It did well in hardcover, and a year later in paperback became my first official US number one. Looking back, I remember it with great affection. For the first and only time, I had a plan and an emotional roadmap. What luxury!

NOTHING TO LOSE

I lived in the south of France for most of 2006, and in March of that year bought a fourteenth-century row house to serve as my office, in the Arab quarter of Lorgues, our local town. It was a tumbledown place—in fact part of it had tumbled down hundreds of years earlier, creating an interior courtyard, which I quite liked. The house was arrayed over three narrow floors, linked by a winding stair. There was a small roof terrace, from which the previous owner had jumped to his death just weeks before. He was a graphic designer, depressed by the onset of Parkinson's disease, which destroyed his ability to work. I bought the place from his widow, and brought in a desk and a chair, and on the first of September I sat down to start my twelfth book.

As always I had no specific plot in mind, but the background to the story had been building for more than three years. The US military had moved into Iraq and Afghanistan in great numbers in March 2003. Quickly their duty settled down to extreme danger when out on patrol, and a measure of boredom and claustrophobia when holed up inside their fortified posts. They passed their downtime watching DVDs and playing video games, and when those attractions were exhausted, they read books, including mine. The posts and bases all had internet connections, and they took to emailing authors, including me.

At first their communications were all brusque banter and trash-talking. They liked Reacher, and saw him as one of their own, but a jokey sense of alpha-male rivalry made them competitive. They said, "We could kick his ass!" I would write back in the same spirit and say, "No, he could kick your ass with one hand behind his back! And his head in a bag!" This went on for a couple of years, from Delta Force in Afghanistan, and the Marines in Iraq, and all points in between. But gradually I noticed my most regular correspondents edging slowly and tentatively toward more intimate subjects.

Which interested me because, years earlier and for unconnected reasons, I had followed a research project at the Imperial War Museum in London, where letters home from British World War One soldiers were being analyzed. (We had donated my grandfather's letters to the archive, and were therefore kept informed.) The scale of mobilization had been so huge there were literally tens of millions of letters. The sample size was unparalleled. One minor and very interesting theme quickly emerged: these were literate people, even the enlisted men. They were the second generation after the 1872 introduction of compulsory education (until the age of fourteen) and their requests for books to be sent out to the trenches revealed a staggering range of interests and capabilities—Greek, Latin, all kinds of novels and history titles and polemics. Back then public education was working, clearly.

But the major theme was psychological. Soldiers found it hard to convey their secret worries. For reasons of peer pressure, they couldn't communicate sideways; for reasons of command presence, they couldn't communicate downward through the chain of command; for reasons of protocol, they couldn't complain upward. They never, ever, revealed their worries to their families back home, especially not to their mothers or younger brothers. There were constant examples (my grandfather among them) of grievously wounded men with limbs blown off writing "Just a scratch, nothing to worry about" letters. There were constant examples of clearly terrified men writing home in a chirpy and confident manner. A lucky few had close friends with whom they could be more open. Those letters were grim.

And those were the kind of emails I suddenly started to get from Iraq and Afghanistan. A tipping point had been reached. Soldiers out there felt close to Reacher; then, as readers often do, they assumed an identity between the character and the author; so now they felt an illusory intimacy between themselves and me. I wasn't their mother or brother. I was a safe harbor, an empty vessel. They felt they could be open with me. I began to receive long, from-the-heart messages. All revealed the same thematic progression. The war was badly run; they were risking life and limb for careless and self-interested politicians;

they didn't know why they were there; they knew the war couldn't be won. In particular I received a message from an infantry company commander, who argued long and eloquently that duty was a two-way street, and that the civilian leadership in the Bush administration was failing the troops in the field they professed to admire so much.

So this was the background I had in mind. My vague intention was to give public voice to those soldiers. I started in the kind of fictional location I love to create—a pair of towns in Colorado that I named Hope and Despair, on a wandering road long ago bypassed by the Interstate system. I let the story develop from there. Hope was a nice place; Despair wasn't. Reacher was thrown out of Despair because of archaic vagrancy laws; on his walk back to Hope in the dark he stumbled over a corpse, literally.

Then a serious family emergency brought me back to New York, and I never used the French office again. Years later I went back to sell it, and found it like a time capsule—a newspaper from November 2006 still open on the table where I had last eaten lunch, and so on. A thunderstorm had fried my modem and blown up my computer. The courtyard had been colonized by pigeons. It was a sad place. I couldn't find a buyer. The locals had no money, and the 2008 crash had dried up second mortgages for Europeans seeking vacation homes. In the end I donated it to my alma mater as a student resource, and took the tax deduction. Better than nothing.

I continued the book back in New York, in a rented penthouse at the top of my building. The family emergency had short-circuited our real estate plans—we didn't have enough space in the city to both live and work. Progress was slow, distracted as I was. But I felt the story was developing in a way I liked. Eventually I needed Reacher to comment on the issues raised by my military email correspondents. I used the long message from the infantry company commander, word for word, as the basis of a fifteen-line speech. (It's in Chapter 63 of the novel.) It came out well, and was by definition completely authentic. It distilled Reacher's dramatic motivations throughout the book. Mixed in along the way was considerable skepticism on Reacher's part about evangelical religion. I thought that was the component that might attract negative comment. I was wrong.

The book was finished, slightly later than normal, in May 2007. Back then I was still a year ahead, so it waited a year to be published, in May 2008. It went straight to number one on the *New York Times* list—my first hardcover number one in America. It was number one in the UK too, and the *Bad Luck and Trouble* paperback was simultaneously number one on both countries' paperback lists—a quadruple number-one week. By a weird coincidence, the day I found out I was on promotion tour and my hotel room number that night was 1111. All good. On top of the world.

Then the hate mail started. The professional critics had been kind, but some amateurs weren't. Random House US is singular among all my publishers in not vetting reader mail before sending it on. Every day for months I would get rubber-banded wads of letters. Most called me an unpatriotic pinko communist, because of Reacher's attitude to the war. Most included that fifteen-line speech, torn out of the book, sometimes shredded, sometimes spat on, several times used as toilet paper. I responded online as often as I could, calling those correspondents chickenhawks and armchair warriors. I reiterated my tour schedule, inviting them to show up and confront me in person. They never did. Just like they never showed up in any war zone anywhere ever. Bullies and cowards.

I never revealed that the fifteen lines they hated so much came straight from the kind of hero their pathetic "Support Our Troops" bumper stickers purported to lionize. That was a private satisfaction. I remain relatively pleased with the book. It's probably not my best, but it's an honest, solid product. The threatened backlash didn't amount to much. I was carpet-bombed with one-star reviews on Amazon, but they didn't have much effect. The next book went straight to number one, too, with increased sales, as have all the subsequent titles. It was a tough couple of years, overall, for personal and professional reasons, but ultimately it was just a tempest in a teapot.

GONE TOMORROW

The internet was in its infancy when I started out as a writer. Some of my friends on the engineering side of television had tried it, but since leaving that industry I knew no one who used it. Eventually, in the spring of 1998, after my first book came out but before my second, and before we moved from the UK to the US, my college-bound daughter asked to get online because she wanted access to something called a "listserv," which would let her get to know some of her fellow soon-to-be freshmen and thereby perhaps make friends ahead of time. So we bought a desktop computer, with a big glass CRT monitor and a plastic case the color of old medical equipment.

Then we bought a dial-up modem and signed up for an AOL account. I sent and received two emails that spring, both to do with the transatlantic purchase of our new house.

We took the computer with us because it had a universal power supply that could work on 110 volts as well as 240. My daughter went off to school and I inherited the computer. At that time I wrote on a separate laptop, so I connected the inherited computer to the modem that came with our new cable TV service, anticipating that email communication might perhaps become an occasional part of my working week. I kept the computer in a closet, and scooted my chair over and opened the door and turned it on once a day to check, in a fairly exact analog of the way I would walk down to the mailbox at the end of my driveway. Some days I would receive or send an email, but most days I didn't. I never visited websites or shopped online. Certainly I never believed anything I read there. Such was my cyber-life at the time.

Then after a year or so my trusty old laptop blew up, and I replaced it with a new flat-screen desktop, and it seemed convenient to hook it up to the modem, out in the open. Out of the closet, so to speak. Over the ensuing months email became more and more frequent until eventually it became the default means of communication. Writer friends started to talk about "online promotion" and eventually I got a website of my own. I visited it rarely, but I suppose even that kind of minimal exposure gradually habituated me to the idea of "surfing the web," as it was called. But still I mail-ordered by phone, read the newspaper, used the Yellow Pages, and followed paper maps when I wanted to get somewhere new. I wasn't so much a late adopter as completely indifferent as to whether I adopted or not. I imagined there might be some potentially interesting stuff online, but I was equally sure there might be in Azerbaijan too, and I didn't want to go there either.

Then I started to hear from writer friends about doing research on the internet. I much preferred my shelves of reference books, which I found I could navigate faster, and which were, for me—illogically, perhaps—invested with far greater authority. But that said, a large part of any writer's research is accidently stumbling over random snippets here and there—every movie you see, every TV show you watch, every person you talk to is a potential source of something. As is, more than anything else, everything you read. And by then I was occasionally reading things online. Even so, I can report with complete confidence that nothing in my first twelve books was researched online, or checked online, or inspired by anything online.

That changed with *Gone Tomorrow*, my thirteenth book, which was entirely inspired by an online discovery.

It happened like this: On July 7th, 2005, three Islamic terrorist suicide bombers detonated themselves in London's subway system, and a fourth on a bus. Fifty-two people were killed, which pro-rata by population was roughly a tenth of US losses on 9/11, but it felt to British people like the same kind of cultural threshold. Because the date worked the same in the UK day-month style as the US month-day style, the atrocity became known as 7/7. But that happened later. In the immediate aftermath there was shock and panic among the intelligence and law enforcement communities. Two weeks later a second subway bombing was prevented. A suspected associate was known to be living in a certain house. The house was watched. A young, dark-skinned man came out, got on a bus, got off the bus unexpectedly, took another bus back in the direction he had come, and then suddenly went down into the subway. Police officers rushed to follow, fearing the worst, and after a brief verbal exchange, they shot the young man dead. It turned out he was not the suspected associate. He was a completely innocent electrical engineering student from Brazil. He had a bed in the same rooming house. That was all. He had changed buses because he had changed his mind about visiting his girlfriend. They were mad at each other.

Two years later, by the summer of 2007, I had become comfortable with surfing the web, on occasion happily spending an hour or two clicking from one link to the next—thereby unintentionally exposing myself to random snippets. And sure enough, one night I found myself reading archived posts from an anonymous message board set up by and for rank-and-file London cops. They all used screen names, so they could say what they wanted without fear of repercussions. I clicked back a couple of years, to their posts from late July 2005, when they were discussing the mistake with the Brazilian student. To give them their due, they were very upset about the error. They were also professionally puzzled. How had it happened? One suggestion caught my eye. One copper had written: "It was because of the List."

I knew British government employees—my father was one—and therefore I knew the capital L in "the List" meant said list must have been promulgated within the department as an official policy document, or as orders-of-the-day. What was in it? I became strangely determined to find out, perhaps as a test of the medium, to settle for myself once and for all exactly how useful the internet could be. I employed all my recently acquired search engine skills, and I tried to think in a not-quite-lateral computer-ish way.

And hours later I found the List, on an out-of-date page on a county police department website in Minnesota, where once it had been posted as a public advisory. It was a list of visual and behavioral clues said to indicate a suicide bomber about to go into action. It had been compiled by Israeli counterintelligence, which sadly had plenty of experience with the issue. The list was twelve points long for a male suspect; eleven for a woman. Point number one in either case was inappropriate clothing. Suicide bombers wear large coats, even in warm weather, to hide the explosive vest. The Brazilian kid in London was wearing a winter down jacket. Not because he was hiding sticks of dynamite, but because England in late July is cold compared to, well, pretty much any month in Brazil.

Right away I was hooked. The discovery gave me exactly the kind of inside-baseball expertise that I—and my readers—love. I knew I had a solid, satisfying start to a story. I knew I had four or five meaty chapters to get the narrative rolling. It was a total gift. I started writing in the fall of 2007. By then we were back from France, permanently in New York City, but our new apartment still wasn't ready yet, so we were still in our original one-room loft, which wasn't ideal for working. So for another year I kept my lease on the duplex penthouse in our building. *Gone Tomorrow* was written in very luxurious surroundings.

Along the way—October, maybe—I went to my brother's place, and my elder niece Katie, then eleven, told me what her new teacher had said about stories, which was that they should always have a bad guy and a good guy. Which advice I was happy to endorse. I asked Katie about the bad guy she had put in her next story, and she told me it was a bad girl named Lila Hoth. Great name, I thought, and promptly stole it. Also in my story, but not Katie's, is Theresa Lee, who is a mystery and thriller super-fan, who bid on a character name in a charity auction.

The only downside to having a great idea to start the book was that it threw into stark relief the fact that I didn't have any ideas at all for the rest of it. But I kept on going, flying blind, and ultimately the rest of the story told itself. In the end I was very pleased with it. It starts well, and then it presses hard, right against the edge of too-much, but it never actually falls off. It was finished in March 2008 and published more than a year later in May 2009. It was a number one best seller all over the world. Recently I heard that it is taught in college as an example of how to open a thriller. Which partly makes me proud, and partly makes me despair about modern standards in education, but mostly makes me agree with the anonymous copper in London: "It was because of the List."

61 HOURS

September 1st, 2008, was a Monday, and Labor Day, the customary end of summer. While the rest of the nation took a well deserved day of rest, I started work on the next Reacher book, as is my habit on that date. I had more than usual to work with—not least a new office. The rehab on my new living space was finally finished during August, so I moved eighteen floors upstairs, and turned my old apartment into a purpose-built and self-contained work space. I put in three desks—the first empty and uncluttered, for handwriting notes and checks and letters; the second with a desktop computer connected to the internet; and the third with a desktop computer not connected to the internet, for writing books. I felt it would aid productivity if I had to get up and physically move six feet to check email or go online—and the plan worked. I would recommend it, although I understand not everyone is as lazy as me. The only non-productive downside to the arrangement was an enchanting view: the Empire State Building, the Chrysler Building, the Met Life clock tower—each at various times the world's tallest building—all right in front of me. But then, gazing into space is as much a part of writing as anything else.

I also had three character names to work with. Over the previous few years, a trend had become established whereby authors offered character names as charity auction prizes. Generally they proved much more lucrative for the charities involved than signed first editions or other conventional ideas. I was a big supporter of the trend. I was keen to help good causes in the most effective way possible, but equally—and selfishly—I was happy to be presented with names, because I often found them difficult to dream up for myself. (All the while living in dread I would be given names ending in the letter "s", which I don't like, because

I think both the possessive alternatives—"s's" or "s'"—look weird on the page.)

I had offered names in three separate auctions that year, and therefore had three winners to accommodate. All had been exceptionally generous, so I wanted to give them good roles. And in all three cases, I found that something about the winners and their circumstances suggested the type of characters they should be. A winner named Mark Salter nominated his mother's name—Janet Salter—and I found myself thinking of her as a noble and principled old lady, determined to do the right thing, no matter how difficult the circumstances. A fellow writer named Andrew Peterson had won a second auction, and I knew him to be a competent fellow, rangy and outdoorsy, and subliminally I thought of him as a local cop—not the chief, perhaps, but a solid second in command. The third auction was won by a guy named John Turner, and he nominated his wife's name—Susan Turner—with the added wrinkle that he requested Susan should have sex with Jack Reacher. I wasn't sure I would or could comply, but again subliminally, I started thinking of Susan Turner in a love-interest kind of way.

And I already had a title. At some point during the summer, *61 Hours* had popped into my head, and was unshakably and irrationally lodged there, in non-negotiable terms. The "61" had to be in numerals, even though I knew it wouldn't easily alphabetize in lists and catalogs and so on. Furthermore, 59 or 60 or 62 were no good—it had to be 61. Vaguely, I imagined the story lasting exactly sixty-one hours—two full days plus thirteen more hours—without any real assurance I could do it, without perhaps Reacher sleeping fourteen hours a night, or perhaps not at all. But such is what passes for my method—start somewhere random, make it up as I go along, and hope for the best.

One downside of that method is that I tend to unconsciously internalize whatever is around me, which often shows up in the weather. I always start on September 1st, most often in New York, when it's usually still very warm. It's no coincidence that most of my books are warm-weather books. My long-time assistant, Maggie Griffin, had noticed and often told me I should write a cold-weather book instead. Which made sense two ways: I was always still writing in the bone-chilling cold of a New York

January and February, when heat and sweat were hard to imagine—would we ever be warm again?—and secondly, as a kid I had loved Alistair MacLean's books, which were often cold-weather tours-de-force. I wanted to try it.

So I did, as the first project in my new office. It was snowing on page one, and from the beginning I incorporated a ticking clock—sixty-one hours to go, sixty, fifty-nine, and so on. I was happy with early progress, and felt the clock added automatic pace—but pace always has a downside, as in I felt I was burning through ideas and incidents at a furious speed. For a long time *61 Hours* was replaced as a working title in my head by *The Book That Wants To Be Too Short*. Ultimately I was saved by the Susan Turner character. I made her Reacher's several-steps-removed successor as commander of his old MP unit, and therefore a long-shot go-to source of information. I decided Reacher would never meet her face to face. Indeed, how could he? She was in D.C., and he was locked down by a blizzard in South Dakota. But they talked a lot on the phone. Just before I wrote their first call together, I happened to talk to Maggie on the phone. She had a head cold, and sounded sexy in a throaty way, and that added to my vague love-interest impression, and in the end Reacher and Turner developed a real phone romance. Which in turn allowed Turner to become more than a supporting character, with third-party scenes of her own, which ultimately defined Reacher's character in the book, as she tried to explain him to herself, as well as helping the length. A win-win.

I tried an experiment at the end of the story, with, ultimately, much less success. My previous life had been in television, where we learned to consider very carefully the exact manner in which narrative was consumed in the real world. In the old days, watching television was a "series" activity, in the sense that full attention was paid to the show, on probably the only set in the house, which probably had pride of place in the living room. Viewers would sit in rapt attention. But a generation later, watching television had become a "parallel" activity—people would watch their shows in the corner of their eyes, while cooking dinner, while on the phone to their mothers, and so on. Attention had become fragmented. Accordingly, we developed a narrative tic—when an important plot point was coming up, first we would tell the viewers we were going to tell them; then we would tell them; then we would tell them that we'd told them. Books, I felt, were different. Although reading time had become somewhat fragmented, concentration itself was usually still pretty good. Accordingly, I wondered if I had stuck to the TV method too long. What would happen if I supplied all the information but let the reader figure out how it all fit together? In other words, in order to avoid over-explaining, suppose I didn't explain at all?

I used that new approach in the aftermath of the big final denouement. Reacher was trapped in an apparently fatal situation. I had supplied enough information for the reader to figure out the only way he could escape. But generally the reader didn't—or didn't want to. People complained either that Reacher was dead, or I had deliberately left the ending hanging. See what you think—maybe it will work for you—but it's an approach I decided not to use again.

The book was published in May 2010 and did very well. Both in hardcover and paperback it became my fastest- and (to that point) best-selling title. There are a thousand factors that influence sales performance, but to this day I credit the color of the jacket. The cold-weather theme showed up as an icy blue—really a baby blue—which proved to be eye-catching and somehow irresistibly attractive. The title made it hard to list alphabetically, but the color of the jacket made it easy to list sales-wise—number one everywhere. (And as a harbinger of things to come, its e-book sales were for the first time statistically discernible, at 3% of the total.)

It remains one of my favorite Reachers, for its characters, and for a certain amount of poignancy, and for the cold, which I thought worked pretty well. It wasn't Greenland or the polar icecap, but I thought Alistair MacLean might have given it a grudging nod.

WORTH DYING FOR

The fall of 2009 was a great one, as I recall. I was comfortably established in my new apartment, and consequently was working comfortably in what had been my old apartment, which was now my new office. We had a beach house in Rye, New York, for weekends, and a supercharged Jaguar to get back and forth. The weather was pleasant. The Yankees won the World Series. All good. I felt the same rhythms and contentments I had ten years earlier. (And I turned fifty-five, which was a relief, because I had always suffered from a vague superstition I would die at fifty-four.)

As always I started my new book on September first. I was still a year ahead. The previous book, *61 Hours*, was completed and edited and tucked away, ready to go into production many months hence, for publication in the following spring of 2010. Before then I intended to have the new one finished, to maintain my habitual and comforting one-year buffer.

It didn't work out that way.

I had left Reacher's fate uncertain at the end of *61 Hours*—an experiment (failed, I thought in retrospect) in which I had hoped to enlist the reader in reviewing the circumstances and coming to a conclusion. Early readers at the publishers panicked a little. Was Reacher dead? Accordingly I decided to make the new book follow on directly from the last scene in *61 Hours*, separated only by a hitched ride out of South Dakota and into Nebraska, a matter of hours. I felt I should show Reacher alive and (relatively) well, as soon as possible. But without backward glances. Reacher isn't the kind of guy who looks back and says, "Phew, that was a close shave." Not his style at all. He just picks himself up and fixes his eyes on the horizon and moves relentlessly forward. I knew I would have to explain his escape, but eventually, not right away.

So I set out writing, as always without a plan or synopsis. The first thing that came to mind was a kind of flash-forward prologue, from the bad guys' point of view. Then, enter Reacher, into the kind of iconic and eccentric location I love so much about the forgotten byways of America. I imagined an isolated motel, styled and gussied up forty years earlier, in a Space Age manner—the Apollo Inn. Reacher orders coffee at the bar. There is one other customer, lugubrious, deep in his cups. The phone on the bar back rings. And off we go.

I wrote on, through the end of the summer heat, into the crisp days of fall, through the Yankees' triumph, and onward through the winter. I did a little specific research. I remember sitting in my room in the beach house in Rye, looking out at the Long Island Sound, learning how shipping containers were invented, and how they are tracked throughout the world. But basically I followed the story wherever it led me. At its core it turned out to be a classic Reacher dynamic—something slightly more layered than just standing up for the little guy, perhaps best explained by a dialog interchange some books earlier, in *Persuader*: during a flashback to his army times, a friend asks why he chose the Military Police, instead of something more glamorous, like Special Forces, or the Armored Branch.

"I like to take care of the little guy," Reacher answers.

"Really?" his friend says. "You care about the little guy?"

Reacher thinks for a minute. "Not really," he says, in a rare moment of introspection. "I just hate the big guy. I hate big, smug guys who think they can get away with things."

Thus the story turned into a contest between Reacher and the Duncan family, who ran their county like feudal lords. Their arrogance was pitted against Reacher's own, to put it honestly, but unprettily.

I finished it before *61 Hours* came out, dead on time, and I was happy with it, but I had no title. My editor, the legendary Kate Miciak, suggested *Worth Dying For*—I don't know why—and by coincidence I had been listening to the English singer-songwriter Dido's live album, and the same three words are in the lyrics of the final track, "See the Sun," and in passing I had thought, "That could be a title." So *Worth Dying For* it was.

Then Kate told me they wanted to switch up the publication date to the fall, not the spring. They felt I was ready for the big leagues—the pre-Christmas sales period, where numbers were much higher, but competition was much stiffer. Which gave us a choice—wait eighteen months until the fall of 2011, or publish six months after *61 Hours* in the fall of 2010.

The feeling was that earlier was better than later, given the ambiguity of the ending, since people needed to know Reacher was still in business. (Plus—never stated, but I'm sure true—Dan Brown had published his follow-up to *The Da Vinci Code* in 2009, which had sold extraordinary numbers, predictably, and in the modern short-termist corporate way, 2009's results would inevitably set the minimum acceptable baseline for 2010, and therefore Random House was keen to drag as much future product into 2010 as it could, to pad the bottom line. (Let 2011 take care of itself!)

I had no objection to the chronology, so *Worth Dying For* came out in October 2010, actually just five months after *61 Hours*. Onlookers assume I wrote two books in a year, which isn't correct. Random House merely burned through the one-year buffer I had previously established. From that point onward

I would be in the same position as any other series writer, with a "just in time" delivery—write, edit, publish, all in short order. I wasn't sure I would like that. There had been a certain psychological comfort in being a year ahead—if Book One came out but wasn't well received, I could know I had Book Two ready and waiting, which people might like better. And theoretically I had a year to fix any evident problems (although I never had). And so on.

Accordingly, on September 1st, 2010, I sat down to write the next one, very aware that I had better "do it once and do it right" (although ironically that had always been my motto). Then I had to break off almost immediately, to go on the road to promote *Worth Dying For*, very shortly after—it seemed—coming off the road after promoting *61 Hours*. Welcome to the second half of your career, I thought.

Worth Dying For did well, even in the pre-Christmas market, reaching number one everywhere. I remember it as an intense, heartfelt story, with a unique singularity in the series so far—Reacher gets injured. His nose is broken. I felt the time was right for him to show some slight vulnerability. Welcome to the second half of his career, too.

THE AFFAIR

This book can be counted two different ways: overall it's the sixteenth in the Jack Reacher series, but it's also the middle book in an odd little sequence of five. The fourteenth book, *61 Hours*, led directly to the fifteenth, *Worth Dying For*, with the stories and the action separated only by hours, and in turn *Worth Dying For* led to the seventeenth installment, *A Wanted Man*, again more or less instantly, with no real gap in the action, which in turn led to the eighteenth, *Never Go Back*, again with no implied delay in chronology.

It happened that way because in *61 Hours* Reacher was snowbound in South Dakota, from where he called his old army unit, to get some necessary information. His successor at his old desk was a woman officer named Susan Turner. Reacher was intrigued by her voice and her manner, and he decided to head over to suburban Virginia to meet her, and maybe take her out to dinner. Because why not? As always, he had no particular place to go, and all the time in the world to get there.

But he didn't get there. Not in *Worth Dying For*, anyway—he got hung up with a problem in Nebraska instead—and I wasn't sure he would get there in the next couple of installments either, which were of course as yet unplanned, untitled, and un-thought-about, but I was enjoying the real-time sequence, and vaguely sensed that I should spin it out for a spell. I liked the momentum, and strategically it meant Reacher wasn't getting a year older with each new book—always a concern for a writer of a series that happily might continue indefinitely.

Thus *61 Hours, Worth Dying For, A Wanted Man* and *Never Go Back* made up a linear quartet, a dogged nonstop journey, as Reacher made his way east, his eyes on the prize, stopping only when obliged to, for (I hoped satisfying) adventures along the way. But as I finished *Worth Dying For*, I had a nagging feeling that I might be giving myself a problem, which was the "eyes on the prize" part. Reacher was looking ahead to Susan Turner, slightly obsessed, and therefore not paying any attention at all to the women along the way.

In other words, he wasn't having sex.

Which was an issue. Reacher's romantic entanglements were important to a lot of readers, especially women readers, who enjoyed his partly carnal, partly courteous, slightly hesitant approach. It was one category among several to be assessed in terms of satisfaction with the story. Fights? Check. Six against one? Check. The bedroom scenes? Check. And there I was, contemplating leaving that last category completely empty, until, presumably, late in the fourth book of the sequence. Given the publication schedule, from the reader's point of view, it might be *four years* between the last interlude and the next.

It was a big enough question that my agent raised it with me. We're both fascinated by the subliminal, real-world reasons books are chosen and enjoyed. (Or not.) But I couldn't just arbitrarily crowbar a dalliance into the dogged nonstop journey. It would make no narrative sense. Reacher was literally fighting his way east, enticed by Turner. Why would he stop and spend time with someone else? And it would be out of character, too—even though he hadn't actually met Turner yet, he would feel some vague notion of honor, or perhaps fidelity, at least to his own personal dream.

So my solution was to step away temporarily from the linear quartet, by stepping away from the current-day narrative. I decided to write another prequel instead. Which I wanted to do anyway. The first book in the series, *Killing Floor*, was set a few months after Reacher left the army, and I wanted to mirror it with a story set a few months *before* he left the army. Maybe it would include the reasons *why* he left the army. Maybe it would show his thinking about exactly how he should live for the rest of his life. And because the story would be completely detached from the current-day sequence, set back at a time when Reacher was younger, more eager, and possibly more carnal than courteous, there would be plenty of logical room for as many steamy scenes as I wanted.

"Good," my agent said. "You should call it *The Affair*. Just to make the point. For reassurance."

So I did. On September 1st, 2010, I sat down at my desk, woke my computer, and labeled a new file "The Affair," instead of merely "Reacher # 16." I liked the title. It had the intended on-the-nose meaning, of course, but it was also a respectful nod toward the mystery genre, where the word by tradition was used for *case,* or *scandal,* or *big enough deal to be worth remembering years later.*

By then my new office was two years old, and running smoothly. I had taken out the residence-appropriate kitchen and replaced it with a narrow counter with nothing but an inset bar-size sink and two drip coffee machines, standing side by side, like a double-barreled shotgun. What used to be the bedroom was now a library, with an Eames chair and ottoman, for laying back and staring into space, an essential but much underappreciated-by-others part of any writer's process. Not that I used it much. I tore into the story and got a lot done in the early weeks. I started at the Pentagon—a fascinating building—with Reacher just back from an overseas assignment and summoned to a meeting. A problem at a base in the Deep South. Off I went.

And then I stopped, because my new fall publication date meant I had to go out on the road to promote the just-released *Worth Dying For*. Promotion tours are lovely, like a warm bath: everyone who comes to see you already likes you, or why would they show up at all? But for the first time I was doing it during my writing season, and I was somewhat aware of the clock ticking. Which I was also somewhat grateful for, because really the whole point of *The Affair* was going to be sex, and I felt subconsciously nervous about diving in. The literary equivalent of performance anxiety, I suppose. Sex scenes are ridiculously difficult to write. Ask anyone—or almost anyone. Some writers are great at it. But not many. Definitely not me.

I got home after giving *Worth Dying For* the best start I could, and got back to work. I read over what I had already done. And there was the answer. By then we were in Mississippi, in a small, no-account municipality, with a huge and semi-secret military base nearby. Special Forces units came and went from there by night, with no flight logs. I knew from visits to locations like that there would be a rail line running north to south, to and from the Gulf ports, and for atmosphere I had already described a giant freight train rolling through the town, shaking the ground and rattling windows. On re-reading, I realized I had given myself a gift. Or at least a possible way to get through the first time Reacher and local sheriff Elizabeth Deveraux went to bed together. A distraction from the biology-textbook aspects.

That distraction eventually had two wider consequences, outside of the story itself. The first was bad, and the second was good. The good came eight years later, when I made a music album with my friends Scott and Jen Smith, who are a band named Naked Blue. The album was called *Just the Clothes On My Back*, and it was about Reacher, essentially. I wrote the lyrics and they wrote the music. At one point, stumped for the next subject, Jen said, "I love the sex scenes in *The Affair*, with the train." So I quickly wrote the words, and the song became *Midnight Train*, one of the best on the album (and possibly the only rock song starting with the word "Then"). It's a showstopper played live. A lot of fun.

The unfortunate consequence was an award nomination in the UK. Usually nominations are to be cherished, but this was for "The Bad Sex Award." The prize was judged on snipped excerpts, not the whole book, and out of context, without the foreshadowing and the set-up, sure, the actual scene itself, standing alone, looked a bit overwrought. Happily, I didn't win.

The book turned out well, I thought, in terms of reverse-engineering Reacher's situation at the start of *Killing Floor*. A lot was explained. It ends with Reacher setting out on foot, on a dusty road to nowhere, as if the series was a Möbius strip, with the sixteenth installment looping back and feeding the first installment. It did well in the marketplace, reaching number one everywhere. Like many of my books, it had a line of dialogue lifted directly from my childhood. In our family we got clean clothes on a Monday. One Monday I was confronted by a small gang of neighborhood enemies as I walked to school. I suspected blood would be involved. "C'mon, guys," I said. "This is a clean shirt." The same thing happens to Reacher on his way to his first date with Deveraux. With the same result: he was embarrassed in the diner by the spray of droplets on the fabric; I got in trouble with my mother. A Möbius strip of a different kind.

A WANTED MAN

This was the seventeenth Reacher book overall, and the third in what turned out to be a four-book real-time sequence of back-to-back stories, which together took Reacher from the snows of South Dakota to the D.C. metro area in his quixotic quest to meet Major Susan Turner, his many-times-removed successor as CO of the 110th MP, his old military unit. It was also firmly in a second category in terms of title, in that it didn't have one until well after it was finished. The previous installment, *The Affair*, a prequel digression away from the miniature four-book series, had been in the first category, in that I had decided on the title before a word of the text had been written. Conversely

A Wanted Man was called "Reacher #17" until well after the last word had been written, whereupon my editor, the genre legend Kate Miciak, combed through the manuscript in search of a resonant phrase or combination of words. At one point Reacher, assuming freedom of movement, is reminded "No, you're a wanted man now," and that was that. I imagine she felt, as editors are wont to do, that as a title the three words worked on several different levels.

I began work on my ritual date, September 1st, 2011, and, as always, I had no plan or outline in mind, but I sensed I wanted to delay the final encounter with Turner a little longer, so I started with a brief page-and-a-half scene, laying out an evident homicide in an abandoned Nebraska water pumping station and a competent but possibly outmatched county sheriff's reaction to it. His strategy to catch the likely perpetrators in such a huge and underpopulated territory was to order up roadblocks on the Interstate, in both directions, on a wide perimeter.

At that point I had no idea what the homicide might be about, but the roadblock response led neatly to Reacher's first appearance, a page and a half later. I wanted to emphasize—to myself, I suppose, as much as the reader—that the action was continuing uninterrupted from the last book in the sequence, *Worth Dying For,* so I consciously cut and pasted part of the last paragraph of that book and used it as the first of Reacher's reintroduction, with just a single character name removed, in order to present it as a clean slate. I prefer not to make readers feel they need prior context to understand the current book, but equally I wanted readers who remembered the end of *Worth Dying For* to feel a sense of continuous action. In one scene Reacher gets out of a van turning west at a highway cloverleaf, sets up to hitchhike east, and in the next scene those actions are reprised, and then continued, until eventually he gets a ride.

I remember enjoying the early scenes in the car that picked him up and I remember vaguely wondering whether I could keep him in the car *for the whole book*. At first it seemed possible, as one conclusion after another unspooled quite naturally. I felt it would be limiting, but a cute technical exercise. But the advantage of not having a plan or an outline was that I didn't need to decide there and then. I could go with the flow, which I did, with regular cutaways to the now-distant county sheriff's investigation, and the

FBI joining in, with Reacher happily speeding away in the opposite direction in the company of a cast of characters that seemed more and more ominous and suspicious with every passing mile. In the end I decided to just sit back and see what would happen.

Meanwhile, what was happening in my real life was that my wife was buying a country house in England. She's from New York, born in the Bronx, raised in two locations in New York State. Her father was an eminent and esteemed theoretical physicist, not a Nobel Prize winner, but close. Two of his best friends were, so that many times as an infant my wife was babysat or minded for the afternoon by Nobel Prize winners. Thus, she grew up part of a hyper-intellectual East Coast culture, typical of the golden age of American science in the 1950s and 1960s. She herself had no taste or talent for science, gravitating instead toward theater, music, dance, history, literature, the history of art, and eventually archaeology.

Her father spent the bulk of his career at IBM, during its glorious and now long-gone period of unlimited R&D budgets. Part of IBM's culture at the time was that such people would spend a sabbatical year somewhere else, once every seven years. For the academic year 1969–1970 he went to Oxford University in England. My wife doubled up on her classes and graduated high school a year early so the whole family could go together. She loved it. Oxford in 1969 was a paradise for an intellectual sixteen-year-old interested in theater, and music, and dance, and history, and literature, and art, and archaeology—and in sex, drugs, and rock-and-roll, of course, which were in full swing by then.

She loved it so much she stayed. At the end of the year the family went home without her. She and I met in school in England a few years later. I was—I hoped—on an opposite trajectory. I was from a grimy industrial city in the English midlands, geographically not far from Oxford but culturally a universe away. I wanted to go live in New York, then, as always, a Mecca for an intending emigrant. I imagined we would head straight there as soon as we graduated.

But I had reckoned without her intense Anglophilia. She wouldn't leave. Then we got jobs and had a kid and were effectively stuck there. But I continued my campaign, and eventually it succeeded, due less to my persuasive powers, I think, than to the way Britain had changed. A person who fell in love with the dreaming spires of Oxford, during the gentle golden postwar consensus, was naturally less entranced with the grubby neoconservatism that had replaced it. Our daughter graduated her English high school in 1998 and we took up residency in America the same month.

A little over thirteen years later the bug returned. My wife started asking if we could get a place in England again. Not to live there permanently. Just as an alternate location, for occasional use. She missed the soft mists and the gentle landscapes and the ancient buildings. What could I say? A month after I started writing this book, she left to begin the search.

She found the place she wanted pretty quickly—an Arts & Crafts country manor on forty-some acres, fifty miles or so southeast of London, fifteen miles inland from the coastal town of Hastings, where William the Conqueror had won the eponymous battle in the year 1066. The house was on the fringe of a tiny village that appears in the Domesday Book that William commissioned, nestled inside a long sleepy sliver of not-very modern-day Sussex that I came to call "The Land That Time Forgot."

In the nineteenth century the railroad companies had favored Brighton over Hastings because of the Prince Regent's influence, way back when. The result was an underserved region useless to commuters. The lack of hustle and bustle included a lack of police departments, which in the recent past had attracted rock-and-rollers looking for country places. Brian Epstein, erstwhile manager of the Beatles, had had a house nearby, as did Keith Richard of the Rolling Stones. Roger Daltrey of the Who still lived in the next village. Paul McCartney himself wasn't far away. Pink Floyd's David Gilmour was close enough to come over for lunch. The house itself was a Lutyens-style beauty, with an overgrown garden that could have been by Gertrude Jeckyll, all set in rolling parkland, with about a thousand oak trees, some of them clearly older than the United States. There was a guest cottage, and a couple of barns. All good.

Except that it was fairly decrepit. The house itself hadn't really been updated since it was built, except for the addition of running water in the 1950s, and electricity in the 1960s. The sole "modern" adaptation was the lone bathroom, which had been installed in the 1970s, with bright orange fixtures. There was no heating. But it had potential, I was told.

The result was I finished Chapter 29 of *A Wanted Man* in New York and then decamped to England, where I began to write Chapter 30, and to supervise the restoration. We lived in the guest cottage, which was relatively habitable, and I worked in its front room, on a temporary table by a window, with a view across our land. On a clear day (relatively rare in England, it has to be admitted) I could see the English Channel, fifteen miles away.

We lived like that for the next several months, my head half full of intricate chases across the American Midwest, and half full of roof tile specifications and underfloor radiant heat. I learned to deal with rural matters, like fencing, and mud, and clay soil, and on re-reading this book ahead of writing this essay it amused me to see those concerns leaking through—the eyewitness to the original pumping-station homicide on page one is eventually revealed to be a farmer, well aware of the cost of fencing, as was I by then, having recruited an ageless eighty-year-old named Les to repair our new boundaries. Reacher's halting steps across uneven terrain were mine, on our exploratory walks, often to our most magnificent oak, situated on what I learned to call our "back field." In the ancient English tradition, we called the giant tree the "major oak," and both it and the cause of our stewardship of it are memorialized in the book's dedication: *For Jane, standing by the major oak.*

The book was finished in April 2012, and the house in May. I lived in it for as long as I could stand, and then returned to New York in about July, leaving its new mistress to run it. I did nothing in August, and started work again on September 1st, on the next book, which—finally!—would see Reacher complete his quest and arrive in Virginia.

A Wanted Man was published later that month and, happily, it was well received and sold fast everywhere. I remember it with affection, and consider it a decent piece of work, not least because I can't really spot the seam between the first part, when my biggest personal decision was what kind of Asian food to order in for dinner, and the second part, when the decision was whether I should apply to the UK government for a subsidy as a sheep farmer.

NEVER GO BACK

Many years ago, the *New York Times* asked me to contribute an article to a how-to-write series. The title of my installment was to be "How to Create Suspense." In it I said that most writing manuals overcomplicate the process. I said that we can reduce the issue to a very basic technique—simply ask or imply a question at the beginning of the story and then don't answer it for a long, long time. People seem hardwired to wait for answers. They do so eagerly, even if they know. They like the gratification of being right.

So in that spirit: there is something unique about *Never Go Back* within the Reacher series. Something happens, or doesn't, that doesn't, or does, in every other installment. I think it's a significant departure but I have never seen it commented on in reviews or online chatter. No reader has ever mentioned it to me. What is it exactly?

I'll tell you later. Much, much later.

Never Go Back was the eighteenth book in the series, which puts it three-quarters of the way through my solo canon, although I didn't know that then. The beginning of my career seemed long ago, and its putative end seemed equally distant. I was in a groove, effortlessly productive, on top of everything. I started the book on September 1st, 2012, at my desk in the seventh-floor office that used to be my apartment, on 22nd Street in Manhattan. It was to be the last book I completed there, although I didn't know that then, either.

There was a lot happening that year. All good. I was living the dream. The rehab of our new English estate was completed in May. In June we went to Los Angeles to see the final cut of the first Tom Cruise movie, *Jack Reacher*, which was based on the ninth novel, *One Shot*. (And which paid for the estate.) We spent part of the summer at our place in France, where our good friends Annie and Louis were celebrating their first grandchild.

Then unexpectedly in October the farm next to the estate came up for sale. It would continue our land westward, and it had four magnificent oak trees all in a line against the horizon, each one easily more than four hundred years old. So I bought the place in a long-distance transaction. Forty-three acres of old England, on the phone. Living the dream.

The rest of October was going to be taken up with promotion for *A Wanted Man*, published that month after completion in the spring. December was going to be all about promoting the movie. After that we planned to spend Christmas in England, and we had a Bermuda vacation booked. Not an untypical year, in terms of distractions. Over time I had learned that actual writing became a smaller and smaller component of an established writer's life. Promotion, PR, general gladhanding, "being a writer," and personal concerns tended to dominate. But somehow, a book had to be written—every year.

The previous three books (interrupted by the out-of-sequence prequel *The Affair*) had been a collective ongoing saga, starting with *61 Hours*, in which

Reacher was making his way cross country to meet Susan Turner, his many-times-removed successor as CO of his old elite unit, the 110th MP. (Note for Reacher trivia buffs: I called it the 110th because 110 was my street address for my first seven years in America.) I decided it was time for him to finally arrive and finally meet her. I felt that to spin out the anticipation any further would be taking the creation of suspense a step too far, very probably counterproductively.

I like to start a story *in media res*, in the middle of things—also a standard writing-manual suggestion and one of the few I endorse. I created a file (pushing my 2012 computer skills to their limit) and named it *Reacher #18*. I typed *Chapter One*. (The easiest two words in any book. To be followed by the hardest.) I suppose to suggest that something had already been happening, that we were truly in the middle of things, I typed "Eventually." Later my editor said it was the only book she had ever read that started with that word.

(But that's not what makes it unique in the canon.)

I suppose in an ideal world Reacher would have strolled into his old HQ and been recognized and remembered and feted. He would have taken Susan Turner out to dinner, over which they would have bonded, and after which they would have connected for life, at the very least as wry best friends.

But that's not my genre. A thriller needs obstacles. And they're hard to find for Reacher. Physical threats are rarely plausible. Readers feel no peril going into such a situation. Instead, they feel pleasurable anticipation, just waiting to see how badly the other guy gets splattered. Non-physical threats rarely work either. Reacher is fireproof against blackmail, bankruptcy, social media, reputation damage, financial calamity, arson, disgrace, cyber threats, and practically everything else. He already *wants* to be homeless. The fears that power most thriller plots are perpetually unavailable in a Reacher story. But even so, that story always needs obstacles.

This time I gave him three. I figured if external pressures would elicit nothing more than a shrug of the giant shoulders, then the uncertainty would have to come from within. Which is also moderately difficult. Reacher is no navel gazer. He just gets on with things. The ground would have to really move beneath his feet, to an extent that left even his colossal self-confidence temporarily unsure of how to proceed.

The first speed bump—the soon-revealed action before "Eventually"—was getting re-inducted back into the army, based on boilerplate in his discharge papers that made an officer with his security clearance a reservist for life. I have no idea if that's realistic—I doubt it—but it doesn't matter. The reader suspects it's all part of some kind of subversive scheme anyway, in which case it might well be made up.

Being back in a rigid hierarchy where instant obedience is expected is obviously a practical problem for Reacher. Being told to go here, go there, do this, do that, obviously gets in the way of the things he urgently needs to investigate. And it's profoundly irksome, too, after an implied decade and a half of total self-determination and footloose freedom.

But it's also a moral and ethical problem. Like most veterans, he's intensely proud of the military and its part in his life but also intensely skeptical of it. As an MP he's seen the worst of it, but to see more still pains him enough to move the ground a little.

The second—and larger—shudder happens when he finally meets Turner under entirely unexpected circumstances that offer not candlelit romance but a desperate bid for survival. Reacher's reaction to her is complex. I tried to capture what I guess most people have felt on occasion. Something about her makes him care what she thinks of him. A new feeling. He recognizes she is facing the greater peril—she could lose what he already lost, fifteen years before, and he remembers how that felt. Her only defense is to be right, which means right in every respect. She must follow the rules of engagement. Therefore, he must follow her. He must do everything right, too. He modifies his behavior. He wants her to be legally safe, of course, but he also wants her to see him as more than just a ragged barbarian. He's not entirely sure why. It leaves him unsettled.

The third and biggest ground tremor happens just after he's re-inducted. He's told that certain entries have been made in his file during his fifteen years of absence. One of them concerns a woman who claims Reacher is the father of her daughter. The kid lives in LA.

A kid would change everything. If true, he would be there in a heartbeat and never leave. He would feel things he had never felt. Instinctively he judges he might like it.

So that was the set-up for the story—conspiracies from the first moment, and big new emotions to deal with. People ask, do I know ahead of time what the ending will be? Truth is I rarely know what the next sentence will be. The story just happens, in real time, right in front of me, and I write it down. It feels like a fragile technique but by then I had learned to trust it. It had worked seventeen times before. No reason it wouldn't for an eighteenth.

Looking back, if I had to be critical, and honest, I don't think it's my best book. The central crime is supposed to be intriguing but it comes across as weird. By far the best part is the possible daughter. I'm the father of a lone daughter and I put myself in Reacher's shoes. How would it feel, at first not being sure, then finding out, one way or the other? That part is solid and I hope it redeems the rest.

It was published in September 2013, just after I started the next one, and it sold very well, with one interesting statistic. E-books had essentially begun late in 2007, and *61 Hours*, in the spring of 2010, had been the first of my books to show even a tiny blip of digital sales—3%, as I recall. Then, astonishingly, just thirty months later, in the fall of 2012, *A Wanted*

Man hit 72%. No technology had ever been tried out more enthusiastically. But 2012 was peak digital for me. *Never Go Back*, in 2013, was in the sixties, the first of a gentle downward trend that in the end stabilized at about 50-50 between digital and paper.

And, of course, three years later, *Never Go Back* became the second Tom Cruise movie, titled *Jack Reacher: Never Go Back*. (Hollywood loves colons.) I thought it a great choice in the character sense, because of the daughter, but also difficult because of Reacher's uncertainties, which are much easier to understand in four hundred pages of a book than in ninety minutes of a screenplay. It came out OK, glossier and more mainstream than the first, and thereby weaker, in my opinion. And it changed a lot of the story, including the part that makes the book unique in the series, which is . . .

There was a clue in this foreword: *He must do everything right too. He modifies his behavior.* Reacher kills no one in *Never Go Back*. He hurts a few but leaves them all alive. Never happened before, never happened since.

PERSONAL

I spent July 2013 in the UK, hanging out at our new farm, supervising the haymaking, tending a hundred oak saplings that had sprouted in a new rewilding margin we had established, fixing my ancient Land Rover—and then escaping the rural cosplay by attending the Harrogate Crime Writing Festival in Yorkshire. I always loved events like that, especially at that time of year—the tsunami of new talent chasing after me always served to remind me I needed to work hard and stay on top of my game. About six weeks from then—when September 1st rolled around—I would need to start the nineteenth installment in the Reacher series, and I would need to make it good. But as usual in July, I had no idea what the book would be about.

Nor did I in August. I flew home to New York, in time to see my friend and fellow writer Michael Connelly throw out the ceremonial first pitch at Yankee Stadium, and a couple days later to get in the last real fistfight I ever had, late at night on lower Broadway. At nearly fifty-nine I had clearly lost a step because, although I won, I got hit and needed eight stitches in a cut eyebrow. That wouldn't happen to Reacher, I thought, and if it did, he wouldn't get stitches—he'd use duct tape. But in my defense I'll point out it was my daughter who made me go to Urgent Care. I was planning to ignore the whole thing, as I do with every health issue.

The stitches meant I couldn't see very well for a day or two and I dropped a glass on my kitchen floor. It bounced, undamaged. It was a classic bistro design from France, where there's a big glass industry, ranging from delicate crystal to tough, utilitarian mixtures. I started musing about unbreakable glass and the subject lodged in my mind.

Also, 2013 was the fifteenth anniversary of my first book tour, which was for *Die Trying*, my second book. No one tours for their first book, because no one knows who you are. Not many people knew who I was for my second book either, it seemed, because attendances were generally modest, except for a number of decent crowds at the specialist mystery bookstores, where word spreads faster and proprietors gin up interest. One of those stores was Murder by the Book in Houston, Texas, where I met a couple who had brought their eight-year-old daughter along. She was a cute kid. Her name was Casey Nice. I saw her again the next year, when she was nine, and the next, when she was ten, and so on. I saw her grow up in front of me, like a series of annual snapshots. At eight, she had to be there, because her parents said so, but at eighteen she had a choice, yet still she came. I felt curiously attached to her. She had grown up with Reacher, and *vice versa*. I decided to use her name for a character in the new book. More on her later.

So, unbreakable glass and a character named Casey Nice. That's what I had in my mind on September 1st, 2013, when I sat down to write. I was still in my seventh floor, 22nd Street office, which had been my apartment until I moved my living quarters up to another apartment on the twenty-fifth floor. I had a battered old Mac desktop on a glass table and a brand-new desk chair that claimed to be super-ergonomic and perfect for posture but which was in fact disappointingly hard and really uncomfortable. Like an instrument of torture. I hauled a soft alternative into place, resumed my normal slumping slouch, and started typing.

For every book, my first decision was always spontaneous and instinctive—first-person narration, or third-person? I said, or Reacher said? I relied on nothing more than whim, really, and on this occasion it came out first-person. Subconsciously I must have felt I wanted to be—and wanted the reader to be—Reacher himself, not merely an observer or reporter. The decision made itself with the fourth word of the book—*Eight days ago my life was an up and down affair.* Not *Eight days ago Reacher's life was an up and down affair.*

The second decision was always how to get him involved. He had no official status and no professional requirement to intervene in any external circumstance. Generally, that meant a significant ask from me to the reader—accept an unlikely coincidence at the beginning and I'll give you a story that makes sense afterward. Usually that was a wrong-place-wrong-time thing. But sometimes I had him sought out and contacted by someone from his past. I typed on and found I was going with the latter option this time. Someone has placed a series of small ads in the *Army Times,* hoping—or expecting—that Reacher will eventually find an abandoned copy somewhere. Which happens right at the top of page two. He's on a bus and two women in uniform get out, leaving a bruised, day-old copy of the paper on their seat. In the veteran-to-veteran personal ad section, there are five words in a boxed column inch: *Jack Reacher call Rick Shoemaker.*

So I was off to the races and ready for the third vague decision: what's this going to be about emotionally? Reacher's motivations had been many and various in the preceding eighteen books—mostly a sense of natural justice, or a dislike of bullies, or a perceived *noblesse oblige* instinct. But this time I felt I wanted a real me-against-you conflict, as in: *This time it's personal.*

Good title, I thought, and I changed *Reacher #19* to *Personal* at the top of the page. Casey Nice showed up pretty soon, as a young CIA staffer, and the hunt is revealed to be for a renegade US Army sniper, once arrested by Reacher as a military cop, now out of prison due to the passage of time. I named him John Kott, which I took from the Polish academic Jan Kott, who many years earlier had written a book I very much admired, titled *Shakespeare Our Contemporary*, which argued that the plays, particularly the histories, could only be fully understood by remembering that Elizabethan England was essentially a police state.

(Bizarrely I once explained Kott's theory to Tom Cruise. We had been invited by the actor Mark Rylance to see his *Richard III* at the London Globe. In the interval Cruise wondered how Shakespeare got away with being so rude about a king and his royal relatives. I told him there had been a regime change. Richard was from the old bunch. The new bunch had violently supplanted them. It was impossible for anyone—even poets—to overstate how awful the old guys were and how much better the new guys were. Cruise got it.)

The unbreakable glass showed up because the sniper's first target had been the French president, in Paris, who survived only because of amazing

French innovations with their bulletproof glass, which wasn't really glass at all, but a super-tough and super-translucent form of aluminum. From a dropped bistro tumbler to a bit of research, to a big strand in the story. That's how my mind works. But more on that later.

I followed whim and instinct as the story developed. Because of the assassination attempt in France, Reacher went to Paris. Then London for the next stop, where the ultimate target seemed to be. I like the challenge presented by writing about England. Normally I'm a Brit writing about America as if I'm a native. For the UK sequences I need to be a Brit writing about England as if I'm a foreigner. I try to see my birth country through Reacher's eyes, which are only semi-familiar with the place. He's a world traveler who has been everywhere many times, yet still finds strangeness. By 2013 I had been away a decade and a half, and every time I came back I would find some new bewildering thing. It's everywhere now, but Britain was the first place I encountered the requirement to pay for the bag they put your shopping in. (Or you bring your own.) I put my own surprise in Reacher's mouth—I have to buy the stuff *and* the bag? What kind of country *is* this? Good, private fun for me.

I decided to stay away from the fancy parts of London that everyone knows—no West End, or Westminster, or Mayfair, or Belgravia. I set the action in the grubbier, less-known parts. Various characters emerged, some of them grotesque. The action developed nicely and built steadily to a climax, perhaps best described in a short story I wrote in 2023—it turned out that the canon shows Reacher hadn't been back to the UK since the events in *Personal* until a random visit at Christmas 2023, the subject of the story, whereupon MI5 is alerted and trace his prior movements: "The sniper suspect was found shot to death in a house in Romford, along with a number of local east London gangsters and criminals, all dead too, from a number of causes, none of them natural." The book was finished late in March 2014, and I was happy with it and thought it came out well, thus illustrating the value of attending summer festivals in order to be threatened by new talent.

The book was published on September 2nd, 2014, and promotion season started right then, thereby disrupting the writing of the new book on day two.

Book promotion hadn't changed much during my career so far, although the scope enlarged as I became more prominent—national radio rather than local, network TV shows rather than local stations, and so on, but the heart of it was always personal appearances hosted by bookstores. One for the 2014 season was in Boston, where I got a great crowd in a separate auditorium. There was a long signing line. (All very different from my 1998 tour!) As I mentioned above, I had used an innovation in bulletproof glass to power part of the plot. I had said it was a French invention, which I thought was true, because of general French domination of the specialty glass industry. And my bistro glass that didn't break was French. But no. Approximately the hundredth guy in the signing line was a distinguished-looking man. He looked like a scientist. He said, "You know the bit about the bulletproof glass? The translucent aluminum? It wasn't French. I invented it, right here at MIT." I apologized profusely, and we parted friends.

Then came something new—for me, anyway, if not Michael Connelly—when the Random House marketing people arranged for me to throw out the first pitch at Yankee Stadium. It was part of an initiative that saw me sign books for players and their families during an afternoon hour, in a lounge with a wonderful buffet laid on by a high-end hospitality contractor. The contractor's event manager came to see me. She had recently graduated college and gotten the job. She lived in Texas but worked wherever they sent her. She was . . . Casey Nice, the real one, all grown up. Her dad came too. It was great to see both of them. It felt like a milestone, all those years later. I did OK with the pitch, as well. Altogether a very happy day, which still makes me think of *Personal* with great affection.

MAKE ME

I finished the nineteenth installment of the Reacher series—titled *Personal*—late in March 2014. Another one in the can—always a good feeling. I checked it through, emailed it to my publishers, and tidied my office for the first time in seven months.

Then the year got busy. First, I moved. I had been living and working on 22nd Street for ten years by that point. My building was a thirty-one-story, four hundred-unit condominium from the early 1980s, built on a site that had been an open-air parking lot, and prior to that a hotel named The Bartholdi, so called because the Statue of Liberty, designed by the French sculptor Frederic-Auguste Bartholdi and a gift to America from the French nation, had been stored in pieces in Madison Park, right across the street. The disassembled icon stayed there many years, while the city scraped up the money to build a pedestal on Bedloes Island in New York Harbor. That accomplished, the statue was erected and the island renamed Liberty Island. The hotel stayed in business until 1966, when it burned down in a catastrophic blaze that held the sad record for the most FDNY firefighter fatalities in a single incident—until 9/11, thirty-five years later.

The smoking ruin was bulldozed and steamrollered, and cars paid to park on the rubble for fifteen years. Then the apartment building went up. By the 2010s many of the original owners had aged out or died, and their heirs had turned their units into rentals, pitched at a price that seemed just right for first- and second-year Wall Streeters eager to live in the hip Flatiron district. Which meant that as I approached sixty, I found myself surrounded by kids technically young enough to be my grandchildren. I would ride down in the elevator with barefoot dudes in pajamas and backward baseball caps, on their way to collect delivery pizza or sushi. There were daughters of D-grade Russian oligarchs, who I didn't want to talk to in case I broke some unspoken Moscow gangster rule and got stabbed with a poisoned umbrella.

Time to move on, I thought. I found a place on Central Park West, on the Upper West Side, with sixty feet of windows on the park. The building was old and quiet, fairly grand, and slightly musty. Just right for an old guy, I thought. The price was eye-watering, but hey, you can't take it with you. I moved in April. I had hundreds of feet of bookshelves built, and some walls repainted. The cost of that work alone was three times the cost of my first three houses put together.

But I loved it there. For the first time in my life I had more shelves than books—for a few months, anyway. I made the back bedroom my office, and closed the door on it, ready for the start of the next novel on September 1st, still more than four months away. Then I flew to England, partly to check on the farm, and partly for my dad's ninetieth birthday, which—although I didn't know it then—turned out to be the last time both parents and all four of their sons were in the same room at the same time.

But mostly I went to continue an informal tour of England's standing stones and megaliths. I was fascinated by them. They were built at the start of the neolithic—the New Stone Age—when, in the blink of a geological eye, nomadic hunter-gatherer groups suddenly froze in place and became sedentary populations farming in fixed locations. Which for the first time ever introduced the entirely new notion that land could be owned. Were the laborious constructions statements of possession? No one really knows.

What really fascinated me, though, was the way they were despised as nuisances by later inhabitants. In August 2014 we went to Avebury, site of the world's largest stone circle. Its diameter is about a quarter of a mile, and a whole medieval village grew up inside its protective ring. Some of the stones were fourteen feet tall and weighed forty tons. And the medieval people hated them. They got in the way of plowing and hovel-building. A relentless effort was begun to remove them. Huge fires were built around them, to make them crack for easier disposal. Those attempts continued for hundreds of years. The cobbled streets of Bath—a nearby and beautiful Georgian town—were paved with their fragments. Even Stonehenge—now one of the world's most revered places—was largely ignored, or derided, or regarded as a stupid, inconvenient obstacle well into the twentieth century. It was still in private ownership as late as 1929, I believe—just a bunch of weird stones in someone's back field. Francis Fukuyama said history ended in 1991—to which we might add that it only seems to have started in about 1931.

I flew back to New York toward the end of August, with the first of September bearing down on me. I had no specific ideas for the new book, but this would be the twentieth time I had had no specific ideas for a book, and it had always worked before. I was confident and really looking forward to starting. I had found that the first day was always a gorgeous feeling—an as-yet unsullied canvas, a world of infinite possibility ahead, nothing to do except sit there and tell myself a story.

Then I was thrown a curveball. A couple of days before I was due to start, I got an email from an English academic named Andy Martin. He was a professor at Cambridge University and an occasional book reviewer for the English papers. He had reviewed a couple of mine, not only favorably, but in a way that suggested he sympathized with what

I was trying to do. His email was a simple question: can I come and watch you write your next book? All of it, from beginning to end?

I wasn't sure how to respond. Watch me? What was his purpose? Partly to write some kind of meta act-of-creation kind of thing, I guessed. To get attention in the journals. He was an academic, after all. Partly to test whether I really did improvise my books, making them up as I went along, with no plan and no outline, as I always claimed in interviews, but which wasn't widely believed. I suspected he wanted to check that out in real time.

What would be my own purpose? I had no need for academic approval. My ego was humming along just fine without it. But it was the twentieth book, which was a happy occasion in itself. Ten times longer than my original contract. Still here. The longest job I ever had. It felt like a milestone. Maybe it should be marked in some way. But this particular way? Many months with some weird guy hanging around, noting things down? I think of writing as show business for shy people. I like to be left alone.

On the other hand, writing is being entranced by why the gerund form works in some sentences but not in others and chasing ineffable rhythms that speed the reader imperceptibly from one sentence to the next. Maybe it would be fun to discuss such things with someone, as they occurred, as the decisions were made, in real time.

But mostly I said yes for shamefully cynical and commercial reasons. There's a big audience out there we weren't reaching—upper-stratum white-collar and professional men, literate, able to afford books, but much more likely to choose a biography of a dead president than a genre novel. But in cultural matters, those men operate inside a permission structure. Maybe a serious book from one of the greatest universities in the world would alter the structure, even if only by a tiny margin. Even if only enough for modest inroads.

I told the guy he better get there fast, because I was starting in a couple of days. I told him I had no plot and no title. Which was only half true by the time he arrived. I had been zoned out on the couch—OK, high as a kite—and I thought of the words *make me*, which I turned this way and that, and saw three ways you could hear them. You could have *make me*, as in *suddenly identify me as an undercover agent or other surreptitious imposter*. You could (at least my generation could) have *make me*, as in *have sex with me*. And you could have *make me* as an aggressive imperative. Stop kicking your dog, you say. To which the guy replies, make me.

Good title, I thought. For some future book. Although, why not this one? It was bound to contain something vaguely relevant. The aggressive imperative, probably. Possibly the sex. Conceivably some kind of clandestine betrayal. Who knew? And really, who cared? Do people really enjoy a book less, just because the title doesn't precisely sum up the content in advance?

So I had a title when Andy Martin arrived. I had told him I start fairly late in the day. We worked out the physical arrangements. My desk was under a window, and behind me on the facing wall was a couch. He sat there, and watched, literally. I opened a new file, and typed *Make Me* at the top, and then *Chapter One* below it. Then I paused.

Do I really make up my books as I go along? The truth is yes, I do. I had been thinking back to a late-evening flight I had taken. It departed four hours late. It was a clear night, and I watched out the window at the amber lights seven miles below. I was seeing everything I would have seen from an on-time departure, but four hours later. A banal and commonplace observation. Millions of people experience the same thing every year. Then I thought, suppose it was a train, not a plane? A closer view of the passing landscape. Suppose I was outside the train, in the landscape? Suppose I was doing something bad that I expected to be entirely unobserved due to the nighttime hour but now might have or could have been observed due to someone else's transportation delay?

I typed *Moving a guy as big as Keever wasn't easy.* Someone was using a backhoe to bury a body. I had no idea who, or why. I had no idea who Keever was, or why he was there, or why he was dead, or what he had wanted. But I was off to the races. The book was underway. The stone was rolling up the hill. I typed on, until the dead guy was safely in the ground and I was done with the first section. I printed it out and gave the pages to Andy Martin as a souvenir and a future reference.

Then we had lunch. I re-read what I had written, adjusting punctuation and a couple of words, aiming to create a distinctive voice and rhythm for the bad guys, to define who they were, and to keep them well separated from the Reacher voice, which I knew would be coming soon. Maybe he was on the train? Maybe he would get out at the next stop? Had he seen something? I wasn't sure, but the day was absolutely illustrative of my method. Andy Martin left after that. I have to say he seemed to sense the atmosphere very acutely. He always got out about five minutes before I was liable to throw him out.

There was no day two—*Personal* hit its publication day and promotion intervened. First up was a network morning show—Andy Martin came with me to observe—and then came days of travel and events. I used to do long, exhaustive (and exhausting) tours—sometimes thirty US cities in twenty-eight days, a couple of two-month round-the-world jaunts—but the unspoken promise behind such marathons was if I did it then, I wouldn't have to do it in the future because, hopefully, the brand would get well established, and ongoing momentum would do the PR work for me. That strategy was paying off. The *Personal* tour was brief and focused. Then I got back to work.

The next few weeks followed the same pattern as day one, with me typing, thinking, scratching my head, typing again, Andy Martin watching, and then getting out just before I punched him in the throat. Then I had to go to Madrid, Spain, where I was due to receive a prestigious award—Andy came with me—and then back to work in New York. The book progressed steadily, day by day, and I began to see what might be going on, what big secret might be festering amid the heartland emptiness. It was January before Reacher (and I) finally figured out the exact issue. Andy Martin saw it happen. Now he knew. He was a witness. I do indeed make it all up spontaneously and in the moment.

The book was finished in April, as I recall. It was a tough plot, with some hardcore nastiness at its center. Certainly, Reacher dished out retribution, but I gave him the sense that while he was winning the battle, he couldn't win the war. That sad nuance added something, I felt. Overall, after checking it through, I was happy with the result. There was some good writing in it.

Andy Martin wrote about his experience in a book he titled *Reacher Said Nothing*. Happily it did what I had cynically hoped it would. It got places I couldn't. Pretty soon Reacher was everyone's darling. Highbrow papers and magazines started talking about the big guy, and they still are. Seven months of varying fun, edge, enjoyment, and irritation paid off. A win all around.

NIGHT SCHOOL

This was the twenty-first installment in the Reacher series. It was supposed to be the last. I had said many times, when asked, that I felt the Travis McGee series by John D. MacDonald was the nearest thing to a progenitor to my own work. I devoured it in the late 1980s and loved it as entertainment but, also, between the lines, I felt I saw what MacDonald was doing, and why, and when, and how, like a secret blueprint visible only to me. The series was an inspiration in terms of its high bar for quality and consistency. There are no bad Travis McGee books. They were lessons in building desperate stakes without showy slam-bang theatrics. Every story was about a defeated everyman (or, very often, a defeated everywoman) who turned to a kind and capable maverick for help. As simple as that. The drama was human.

MacDonald wrote twenty-one installments, and then he died, from coronary problems, at the young age of seventy. The number twenty-one stuck in my head. As soon as it became obvious that the Reacher books were shaping up into a potentially durable series, I would be asked how many books I planned to write. In the early days—two or three books in—it was a fairly meaningless question, because the answer depended on numerous circumstances entirely outside of my control. Nothing in any branch of the entertainment business is predictable or certain. But for the sake of saying something, I would always answer, "Twenty-one, like John D. Macdonald."

Then I started to believe it. I know that sports analogies are usually best avoided, but the events of September 6th, 1995, were on my mind. On that date, Cal Ripken Jr. broke Lou Gehrig's record of 2,130 consecutive baseball games played. I wasn't happy. Not just because I'm a Yankees fan, not an Orioles fan, but because Ripken was not an ultimately superior talent, or a better man, or a tougher guy. The record was broken only because Gehrig had come down with a tragic and fatal disease. I felt Ripken should have matched the 2,130 number and then sat out a game, as a mark of great respect, as a hat-tip to fate and karma. I wished he had. I felt that would have been much classier, and much better mannered.

Sauce for the goose, sauce for the gander. I started to think I should match MacDonald's twenty-one and then stop. Because he had died, not retired voluntarily. Ridiculous, I know. Irrational and irrelevant. But the notion was implanted. Not exactly an elephant in the room, but at least a moving shadow in my peripheral vision. In retrospect I can see its subconscious influence. Book number twenty—*Make Me*—ended with Reacher and his love interest Chang leaving the scene together, literally driving off into the sunset, side by side. That had never happened before. It hinted at the possibility of a settled and contented future. Then, somehow, implacably, book twenty-one emerged in my head as absolutely needing to be a prequel. I felt it shouldn't advance the current-day narrative any further, because the possibility of a settled and contented future was a good place to leave it. I felt instead the last book should act as a kind of

Möbius strip, looping back to the beginning, as if its momentum would launch *Killing Floor* all over again.

As always, I had no plan, no outline, no specific ideas, but somehow I knew for sure I would be writing about, say, 1996, not 2015. But that was September's problem, still to come, some months away.

The spring and summer of 2015 were a mixture of pleasures and problems. The pleasures included time spent at the UK farm, pruning roses, clearing thistles, tending my oak saplings, polishing my antique Jaguar, trying to make my antique Bentley run. We went to Amsterdam for a week, which was fun. I went to Book Expo America at the Javits Center in New York, where *Make Me* was pre-launched. We went to Maine for a vacation with our daughter. We went to Norway for our fortieth wedding anniversary. All good.

The problems included a big decision in May. My beloved soccer team, Aston Villa, made it to the F.A. Cup Final, to be played at Wembley Stadium in London, a Super Bowl- or World Series-level accomplishment. The club—generously deeming me a "celebrity fan"—offered me tickets. The team hadn't won the prestigious trophy since 1957, when I was two and a half. Now I was sixty. A once-in-a-lifetime opportunity, with a team like mine. I really wanted to go. I knew I would forever regret it if I didn't. But equally I knew they would lose if I actually showed up. Such are the certainties in any sports fan's head. I went, with my brother Andrew, and sure enough we lost badly, 4-nil to Arsenal. Oh, well.

The other big problem was an IRS tax audit. It seems every nation needs a scary agency, relentless, implacable, all-powerful, all-seeing. In the old Soviet Union, for instance, it was the KGB. In contemporary America, it's the IRS. But I wasn't fearful.

I'm always honest with my taxes; I operate an *if in doubt, leave it out* approach when I'm unsure about an expense or a deduction; I have a law degree; I'm very articulate; I'm a world-class pedant; and most of all my dad was an auditor for the Inland Revenue, the UK equivalent of the IRS, so I grew up speaking their language. I know how they operate, and I recognize their stressors and their insecurities. In fact, just for fun, I called the auditor at the outset with a Reacher-style message: go ahead if you choose to, I said, but be warned—you'll lose. I'll beat you like a rented mule. You'll be embarrassed and humiliated but, hey, it's your call.

The guy chose to go ahead, of course. I didn't use a lawyer or an accountant. I enjoy personal battles with bureaucracy. In fact, I think they're seriously important. If we ordinary folk let it get to the point where a mere accusation from on high becomes the functional equivalent of a guilty verdict, then we're many steps closer to a police state. I believe it's civically important to put the accuser through the forensic and judicial hoops every single time. Plus it's a winning strategy.

Almost inevitably the state screws up on some part of the procedure. I have disputed every single speeding ticket I have ever gotten and I have won every single time, most recently in suburban New York, where I requested the reporting officer's official affidavit, a legal right almost no one avails themselves of.

In the first paragraph, he said I was driving an Infiniti. In the second, I was driving a Saab. Well, which was it? Case dismissed! (Too long a story for this 2015 foreword because the matter stretched onward well into 2017, but I did indeed beat the IRS in the end—and a close examination of the if-in-doubt issues left the government owing me half a million dollars. The auditor was demoted as a result. Sad for him but, hey, he had been warned.)

That process was rumbling through its earliest stages in July and August, as September bore down on me. I planned to start the new book on the first, as always.

The idea of a prequel was a given by that stage, but I felt vaguely reluctant to do an in-the-army police procedural. I had done that in *The Enemy* (the eighth Reacher book) and *The Affair* (the sixteenth) and I wanted to try something less structured.

Middle Eastern terrorism was an evolving threat in the 1990s, and governments around the world were responding with free-form, all-hands-on-deck, "hair on fire" approaches. I imagined an ad-hoc multi-agency task force thrown together in a panic. Maybe CIA, NSA, and the FBI would be included, plus the Army, because maybe the problem involved US bases in Europe. Who would represent the Army? Well, Reacher, of course.

We finished our anniversary jaunt to Norway late in August, and I flew back to New York on the 31st, ready to start work the next day. I almost didn't make it. I had booked on the British Airways flight from London City airport, departing about eight in the evening. That service was operated by small Boeing

737s with all business-class seating, about thirty-some pods in total. When flying west, battling the jet stream rather than benefitting from it, the small fuel load meant the plane had to stop in Shannon, in the west of Ireland, to top off the tanks for the long transatlantic haul. The upside is that Shannon has US customs and immigration, so we would arrive at JFK as domestic passengers. Slower en route, but quicker at the far end.

But that night the refueling did not go as planned. What they pumped in sprayed right out again through a leak. Something had come loose during the landing. There were no parts in Shannon. Something would have to be flown in, perhaps from Seattle. The airline announced it was finding us a hotel for the night. The plane had been less than one-third full—only ten passengers or so. August 31st was a public holiday in Britain, so no one was returning from actual meetings. By about nine thirty we were on a bus south to Limerick. The hotel had agreed to keep the restaurant open, so we could have dinner.

What followed was a lovely meal and a fun couple of hours. There seemed to be an unspoken agreement not to talk about work. We were just ten complete strangers, late in the evening, alone at a big table in a dim and deserted dining room. It felt like the set-up for a murder mystery. My only problem, because I had homes at both ends of the journey, was that I had no overnight stuff with me. No pajamas, no Dopp kit. But I managed. In the morning, I called British Airways for an update. I had flown a lot, and I had learned to listen—not to what they say, but how they say it. And the tone wasn't good. It was clear the plane wasn't going to be fixed that day. So I rebooked on United and got out of there. I got home to Central Park West about nine in the evening on September 1st. Three hours left to make a start on my traditional day.

I typed: *In the morning they gave Reacher a medal, and in the afternoon they sent him back to school. The medal was*

And then I stopped. I'm a very linear writer—I can't leave a gap, or an "xxx," for future completion. My method means every sentence is essentially created by the previous sentence, so I can't move forward until the previous sentence is properly in place. And I didn't know what medal Reacher had been awarded. What kind of thing might he have done to earn it? What medal would that get? I didn't know yet, so I stopped for the night. Just twenty-one words (there's that number again) but the book was officially underway on September 1st, for the twenty-first consecutive time. Good enough, I thought.

The next day was a blast. I raced through the opening sequence. As always, I was making the story up as I went along, but in turn the story itself was about people making things up as *they* went along. The alleged school Reacher was ordered to attend wasn't a school at all but instead was indeed an ad-hoc multi-agency task force thrown together in a panic, free-form, freewheeling, and improvised. I never pretend to be a realistic writer, but even so I often hear the voice of my conscience asking, is that how it would really happen? Would they really do it that way? Is that even *remotely* likely? But the nature of the story I was writing silenced those doubts. Anything goes, in a situation like that. I was liberated. My conscience kept quiet. I did a couple of thousand words that day, and the next, and the next. For two solid weeks the story poured out and I made maybe the best progress I have ever made.

Then the year slipped back into a familiar chopped-up pattern. I toured for the launch of *Make Me*, which included a week back in London; then I went to New Orleans to visit the set of the second Tom Cruise movie, *Jack Reacher: Never Go Back*; then back to the UK again for a fundraiser to help the Harrogate Festivals people; then Stockholm for joint appearances with Andy Martin, for both *Make Me* and Andy's book *Reacher Said Nothing*; then New Orleans again, to film my cameo scene in the movie; then Key West in Florida for a literary festival. For four months I wrote when I could, two days here, three there, with the occasional luxury of a whole week uninterrupted.

From late January onward the schedule calmed down, by which time I had rolled the stone all the way up the hill and it was poised to roll down the far side unimpeded. There is no better feeling than seeing the finish line ahead and barreling recklessly toward it.

In particular, I was enjoying the bad guy. I hadn't wanted to make him a standard-issue evil genius. Instead, he turned out to be a normal guy, shifty, shady, somewhat hapless, sometimes incompetent. A bit like one of MacDonald's defeated everymen, but Reacher's opponent, not his protectee. On the surface an easier target than usual but the action was in Hamburg, Germany, where Reacher was more than ever a fish out of water, with local sensitivities to navigate.

I wrote the last word in March 2016, and I was pleased with the result. It was a good, solid book, I thought. Was it the last ever? It would have worked as such. Its Möbius-strip momentum carried it into Reacher's final spell in the army. His future footloose life was clearly visible ahead. But my diary had an upcoming lunch date with my publisher. I knew what was on the agenda. But that's a story for the next essay, not this one.

THE MIDNIGHT LINE

My semi-superstitious instinct to make *Night School* the last of the Reacher series didn't survive a lunch with my publisher. In fact, it didn't survive a previous week of personal introspection. I was fantastically lucky. The decision whether to write or not to write the twenty-second installment of a globally best-selling thriller franchise was the ultimate first-world-champagne problem.

I had a great life. My readers had built it for me. They loved Reacher. They wanted more. I owed them everything. So, yeah. And actually . . . there *was* something on my mind. I thought it might make a good story. Not exactly an idea, but an angle. A point of view. Something I wanted to say.

My publisher knew none of that, as we sat down to lunch. I could tell he was nervous. I didn't want to be a diva, so right away I said, don't worry, I'm going to do a few more. After that, it turned into a regular lunch. Good conversation and good food. And great champagne. He had ordered it before I told him.

So the year 2016 followed a familiar pattern after all. Normally April through August were non-writing months, filled with both personal and writer-related trips and commitments. Slightly unfamiliar was the stature of some of the writer-related stuff—very *haute monde* compared to normal, due to the academic Andy Martin gamble I had made in 2014 and 2015. It was paying off. I did events at both Oxford and Cambridge universities in the UK and was interviewed for a long feature by *The New Yorker* magazine in the US—all three representing very rarefied air for a genre writer. Although it has to be said that the media landscape had been changing for books, first in the UK, later in the US. It used to be that serious broadsheet newspapers tailored their coverage of everything else to satisfy their readers' interests—political, financial, economic, social, and sports coverage was all aimed right where they lived.

But books were different. Book reviews seemed aspirational, as if the papers were saying, "Hey, we know you don't actually *read* the books we mention, but we figure it makes you feel good if we all pretend you do." As if sports coverage ignored soccer and cricket in favor of polo and chess. Then, gradually, some measure of capsule "guilty pleasures" coverage started up for the books people actually *did* read, which developed into serious analysis of genres previously considered profoundly unserious.

Finally it was admitted that captains of industry, and bankers, and lawyers, and professors read and enjoyed John Grisham, Stephen King, Michael Connelly—and me. We ourselves were asked to comment on things as if we were authorities. I made a radio program for the BBC about John D. MacDonald, for instance. I went to Sweden to be on a rarefied-air TV show, to talk about crime fiction, alongside a famous political commentator talking about the rise of authoritarianism. And so on. The democratization of culture, some said. Its debasement, the hold-outs countered. Plain common sense, I thought.

The biggest difference for me in 2016 was that for the first time in twenty-two years I didn't start the new book on the first of September. Instead, I started it early, in the middle of August, and I had the opening chapters nailed down before September rolled around. We had booked a trip to the Orkney Islands, off the north coast of Scotland. The only dates we could get straddled my usual starting day. We wanted to go there to see the greatest concentration of neolithic remains in the world—stone circles, stone houses, all kinds of magnificent artifacts.

Five thousand years ago what became Britain was upside down—power and influence lay in the far north, not the southeast, where eventually the upstart Londinium was founded by the Romans, some three thousand years later. The archipelago is exposed to the Atlantic, and therefore perpetually windy, which means few trees grow there, which means prehistoric builders used stone, which survives indefinitely. The oldest known remains are a neolithic farmstead named the Knap of Howar, on an island with the beautifully romantic name of Papa Westray.

We had a great two weeks there, roaming around in a rented Nissan, taking ferries, visiting one spectacular site after another, including one my wife had helped excavate when she was an archaeology undergraduate, forty-three years previously.

Then I flew back to New York and got back to work. I already had a title for the book. My brother Andrew used to work in the telecoms business and earlier that summer had told me about an installation they had once discovered where, due to a software glitch, calls on one particular phone were free, anywhere in the world, from late in the evening until dawn. They called it the midnight line and made lots of use of it.

Good title, I thought. I didn't know how or if it would fit with the story, but—as with *Make Me*—I wasn't really worried about that. By definition, readers know the title first and the content second, and very few of them think back afterward and object if the two don't match up exactly.

Unusually, I also had two ideas for the book, not detailed or definitive, but useful as a guide. The first was a narrative engine created by a straightforward ring quest—operating in reverse, in fact, in that the ring was discovered at the outset, and the quest would be for its owner. In January, while I was still writing *Night School*, I had gone to Key West for a literary festival, where I met the son of one of the organizers.

He was an infantry major in the army and had just gotten back from a tour in Afghanistan. His next posting was to West Point as a military history instructor. (Army officers are generally pretty smart people, with more than one string to their bow.)

He invited me to visit, for a behind-the-scenes tour, which was fascinating. I met numerous cadets, all terrific people, especially the women. I sat in on a history class, and my friend invited me to set a military history question for an exam. (For the record, my question was: Explain in one sentence why the allies won World War Two. The answer I was looking for was: Whereas immediately and instinctively FDR, Churchill, and Stalin understood that the war would be one of mass industrial production, Hitler did not. See the historian Richard Overy's work for more than one sentence on the subject.)

But what turned out to be the crucial point of the visit for me was a display of West Point class rings. I learned that West Point was the first educational establishment to come up with the idea of class rings; that graduating cadets design their own, on an individual basis; and that they are highly prized by their owners as evidence of survival of a regime that basically spent all day every day trying to make every one of them quit and go home. That approach was held to produce the most tenacious officers, and was as true as ever in 2016, especially for women.

So I started with the notion that Reacher would find a West Point class ring, tiny in size, therefore a woman cadet's, maybe in a pawn shop. Being a West Pointer himself, he would understand only a very serious problem would have made her give it up. Therefore, he would seek her out and offer his help. Simple as that.

What was her very serious problem? For the last several years we had been hearing about the opioid epidemic. Synthetic heroin, at first principally OxyContin, was being marketed as an effective painkiller. Which it absolutely was, like its parent morphine had been. But it was also viciously addictive, as expected. Genuine patients, perhaps victims of accidents, at first appreciated the palliative qualities, but soon became horribly dependent. A huge new population of drug addicts was created. An above-ground medical infrastructure catered to them to a generous extent but, when their cravings grew unmanageable, they turned to an underground criminal infrastructure for relief.

Most crime fiction on the issue was on the latter subject. Bent doctors, pill mills, truck hijackers, chemistry labs, coke dealers looking to branch out, meth dealers looking to fight them for it. Plus sly Pharma companies making out like bandits, sinister cartels eyeing up the business, and law enforcement battling all of them. The addicts themselves were mere ciphers—useful only to follow to some dealer's address, for the next clue.

I didn't want to do that. I wanted to write it from the addict's point of view. Which I couldn't, really, because these are Reacher books, and Reacher isn't an addict. But would he be sympathetic? Yes, he would, because he does what his author tells him to, and I am. He would start by asking why people have to live such hard, hard lives that an opioid high was the best feeling they would ever have. He would have seen how different people have different vulnerabilities, almost on a molecular level.

Me, for instance. I don't get colds or the flu—more than thirty-five years since my last bout with either—but I get addicted easily. My molecules murder some things but enthusiastically embrace others.

So it would be a sympathetic point of view, and the addict herself would be a leading character. I wrote on and made good progress. The story had started out in Milwaukee, Wisconsin, and seemed to be headed toward Rapid City, South Dakota. I imagined it might then loop back east and maybe end up near Chicago. Or downstate Illinois, perhaps. Opioid addiction seems to be as rural as it is urban.

Then the geography changed totally. In October I moved to Wyoming. It's hard to explain why. My brother Andrew moved there from Chicago; we visited, and were strangely attracted. Part of it was an immigrant thing—I love New York City but in the back of my mind I was always slightly restless. Was there somewhere else worth trying? Was there somewhere I would like more? In particular, I wanted a total contrast. The Upper West Side of Manhattan has a population density around 100,000 people per square mile; Wyoming has a population density of basically zero. It's physically bigger than the entire United Kingdom, where I'm from, yet has a population smaller than Louisville, Kentucky, thinly spread over all those square miles. A vast, empty, tawny landscape.

So the story moved west with me. From Rapid City, South Dakota, the action carried on along the Interstate corridor until it hit the foothills of the Rockies. I changed some place names, but I was writing about my new neighborhood—a zip code larger than Manhattan, with fourteen residents.

In retrospect I see how the novelty gave me energy and focus. I finished the book in April—still bleak midwinter in Wyoming—and I count it as one of my best. Maybe *the* best. It was published in the fall of 2017 and was well reviewed. For months I got mail from people grateful for the sympathetic, human approach. Some messages came from healthcare professionals dealing with the catastrophe. I was very happy to get them, and happy to feel I was helping, however peripherally.

I was left with an irony—it was perhaps my best book, but it was one I might never have written.

PAST TENSE

By the middle of November 2016, I was making pretty good progress on *The Midnight Line*, the book before this one. As I mentioned in the previous essay, it was written mostly in Wyoming. What I didn't mention was I took a week back in New York in mid-November to do a couple of things there, with a trip to Ohio for a library fundraiser sandwiched in between. Almost all writers are devoted supporters of libraries. Almost all of us got our start there, as kids, intoxicated by a place where they would give you any book you wanted.

I flew out of LaGuardia, traveling light. A small bag for a one-nighter. I put it on the X-ray belt and put my pocket stuff in the dog bowl. Cigarettes, lighter, wallet, keys, phone. Which right then started to ring. I grabbed it back out and answered. I thought it might be my publicist, with a change of plan. But it wasn't. It was my brother David, calling from Britain. He said, "Dad died."

I said, "OK," and he rang off. This was a typical conversation with most of my family. Short, sharp, to the point, nothing wasted, not time or money or international cell phone minutes, and certainly not emotion or feeling. I waited for my phone to come out airside, in a second dog bowl, and I walked to my gate.

There was no rift between me and my father, no dramatic estrangement. I saw him from time to time, whenever I could. I liked him well enough, and he liked me well enough. I admired him, in many ways. He was six when the Great Depression began and had a pinched, narrow, self-denying childhood, made worse by a dour and crazy brand of Ulster Protestantism imposed by the community. Then he volunteered for the British army. (There was no draft in Northern Ireland, because of political sensitivities.) The eleven months and two days between D-Day and

VE Day fit symmetrically into the year he was twenty. He was a captain in charge of an engineer company maneuvering with the armored divisions. Then he raised a family in bleak postwar austerity, and made sure we could all read, swim, and drive a car. His three main duties as a parent, he said.

When in turn I was six, the 1960s began. My life was completely different. I lived for pleasure. Sex, drugs, rock-n-roll, and stories. He disapproved of all of it. Mixed in with the disapproval was sheer bewilderment. For years I thought he thought the moral choice between pleasure and duty was so crystal clear that it was astonishing that anyone could miss it. Eventually I saw it didn't get as far as a choice. Duty was his only reality. He didn't really know what pleasure was. He was never allowed any. He was a decent guy, hopelessly stunted by his upbringing and his lived experience.

So we didn't have much in common, and we were never close. He was in a bad state the last few years, and he was ready. We all were. Which is why I got on the plane. For once he would have approved. I had committed to an event, and duty came first, come what may. It gave me some good lines in Ohio, though. "How are you?" people would ask. "Not too bad," I would say, "My dad died." "Oh, I'm so sorry. When?" "This morning."

Nine months later *The Midnight Line* was long ago put to bed and I was two weeks away from starting the next book. As usual, I had no specific ideas. No detailed plan, no bullet-point outline. But, inevitably, I had spent some time thinking about my dad. Not in an emotional or sentimental way—that stuff didn't fly in my family; in sixty-two years he had never said, "I love you," either to me or anyone else within earshot. Instead I thought about how little I knew about him. How much do we really know about anyone? We know the bare bones of biography but can never really know how another feels, or thinks, or experiences things, or what exactly they have done, or not done.

That would be the theme of the new book, I decided. Reacher and his dad. Plus I had two names firmly fixed in my mind. We had driven from our home near Laramie to the Tetons—an eight-hour diagonal trip through Wyoming—and on the way had stopped for lunch in DuBois, an old cowboy town that still had wooden sidewalks. In one of them someone had used a hot poker to burn a list of names. I don't know who or when or why. The first name was Shorty Fleck, and the last was Patty Sundstrom. Somehow irresistible. They were going to be characters for sure. I figured Reacher would be randomly in New Hampshire and he would see a signpost to Laconia, which he knew was his father's birthplace—the bare bones of biography—so on a whim he would detour and check it out. Meanwhile Shorty Fleck and Patty Sundstrom would be in the area, in some kind of trouble, and no doubt Reacher would intervene and help them out. That ended up being a pretty substantial outline, by my standards.

I got to work on the first of September 2017, in my back bedroom office on Central Park West, in New York. Not that the back bedroom had a view of the park. A brick wall, mostly. The first sentence I wrote turned out long and elegiac, with a real end-of-summer feel, and it mentioned birds in the sky.

Since my method means every sentence is essentially created by the previous sentence, clearly I would now have to name some birds. So I asked my wife, who knows birds the way people know baseball, to tell me what birds would be migrating south through the New Hampshire fall skies, and she gave me a list, which I rearranged for rhythm and cadence, so then I had two pretty good sentences. Plus, I realized, a still-functioning subconscious, because I suddenly remembered a brief mention of Reacher's dad I had made in a much earlier book.

He was a Marine infantryman, who as a group are not the softest people you will ever meet. Except they usually are, about some other random thing. I had called Reacher's dad a stone killer and, to illustrate the duality, I had added that his passion was birdwatching.

Birds had showed up in the first sentence, and the second. Obviously that was going to be a running thread. Meanwhile, Shorty and Patty had to be introduced. I loved them both from the start. I made them Canadian, therefore nice, according to literary convention, but hapless, he more so than she. The first sentence had been languid but the story came pouring out like a river. I worked twenty-five days straight and then I broke off for the real-life outcome of a coincidence so blatant it would have been laughed off the page by any editor in town.

Way back in the 1960s, part of the rock-n-roll component in my life was supplied by the original incarnation of Fleetwood Mac, led by all-time-great guitarist Peter Green. Who had a breakdown and disappeared. And then reappeared many years later, in a bad state, so the modern-day biz rallied round and recorded covers of his songs, so he would get songwriting royalties to help with his expenses.

The CD was called *Rattlesnake Guitar*. It came out in 1996, before I was a writer. I really liked it, especially a track by a band called Naked Blue. Loved it. I had never heard of them, but I kept an eye out, and sure enough there was an album, and a second, and I grew to be a big fan. In a certain mood, they really hit the spot.

Jump tracks and fast forward five or so years and I had become a writer. I was just a few years in, still in a largely pre-digital era, and I would get occasional fan letters. One was from a guy in New Zealand. His name was Marcus. I wrote back and we're friends to this day. Another was from a couple in Baltimore. I wrote back to them, too. They said they were coming to New York for work, and how about coffee or a beer? I said sure, where and when? We're playing a club, they said. We're a band called Naked Blue.

The beer turned into many. Scott and Jen Smith. Fabulous musicians and even-more fabulous people. Obviously we immediately agreed to make an album together, somehow combining them and me. I would write the lyrics, and they would write the music. But they were busy, and I was busy. It took us about fifteen years to make it happen. But eventually it did.

After twenty-five straight days on *Past Tense*, they came to stay the weekend. We were determined we would write the songs, and we were determined we would get the album done. And we did. It was awkward for about thirty seconds because I was their fan and they were mine, but we got over it fast and wrote song after song on the spot. They wanted Reacher-style themes and I wanted Jen to sing them. I figured the contrast between the tough-guy sentiments and the sweet purity of her voice would be intriguing. And it was. I loved the result.

The CD was called *Just the Clothes on My Back* and, as an homage, it has a swampy version of Howlin' Wolf's "Killing Floor," the only non-Smith-Smith-Child composition on the record. Later we toured it to bars and clubs, playing live, getting paid.

They left after that initial session and I got back to the book. The putative outline was in danger of falling apart. For a long time it felt like Reacher's intervention wasn't going to be necessary. Patty and Shorty were doing just fine on their own. But I couldn't have two separate, completely unconnected stories. Could I? No, wouldn't work. I wrote on, hoping for the best.

I finished it in March 2018, and I thought it was solid. It was gruesome in parts, but it was mostly upbeat, and it had a surprise (I hoped) for Reacher, about his dad, at the end. It was published that fall, and it did well. I look back on it as a very happy experience. Even though I got a second call from my brother David in Britain while I was writing it. Now my mother had died too. But, really, she had gone years before, hopelessly lost to dementia. She didn't know who I was, just as I would never really know who she had ever been.

BLUE MOON

This book started with a toothache. I had spent the non-writing part of 2018 mostly in Wyoming, with side trips to the UK, France, and Poland—the latter at the request of my Polish publisher, who wanted me to do a couple of events there, which turned out to be fun. I had never been to Warsaw before, and I would recommend it, even if only for the soup.

The French visit was the last time I stayed at our house there—we sold it shortly afterward, a matter of some regret, but not too much. I need to be immersed in language and, although I can manage French fairly well, the sheer effort of keeping up with a subtle four-hour dinner conversation exhausted me to the point of seizure.

The UK component was the usual time on the farm—haymaking, striding about with my walking stick, pretending to be part of the landed gentry.

By mid-August I was back in the Wild West, enjoying the brief summer, hanging out, sowing wildflower seeds, more in hope than expectation, given the bone-dry climate, and generally relaxing. Then in the middle of August a molar got sore.

I had neglected to register with a doctor or a dentist, despite having lived there nearly two years by that point, so I checked online for the names of Laramie dentists. One of those names was Shevick. In the end I went with another guy, but the name Shevick stuck in my head. That's how it is for writers—this one, anyway. Sometimes I hear a name, and a whole personality sparks to life. In my head I saw a tired but valiant old man beset by problems and negative circumstances.

The nature of his problems drifted into focus as something to do with healthcare, probably. After all, I had found him because of a toothache. Not his own healthcare, though—he was probably too stoic and self-reliant to worry about himself. Possibly his daughter's? Maybe she couldn't pay her medical bills. Maybe he was borrowing money and getting into trouble with loan sharks.

I had the title well ahead of time, because *Blue Moon* is a song I love, for its tune, certainly, but mostly for its first-verse lyric, which always struck me as Reacher-esque: *Blue moon / You saw me standing alone / Without a dream in my heart / Without a love of my own.* Plus, I figured it would be nice if, once in a blue moon, something worked out well for poor old Mr. Shevick.

All that was what I had in my head when I sat down to start, on the first of September 2018. I began with the bad guys, who I made Ukrainian and Albanian, two gangs duking it out in an unnamed city. Later Ukraine would become the object of worldwide sympathy and concern, but at the time I wasn't pleased with the place. There was a huge piracy operation there, ripping authors off with copied e-books. John Grisham and I were nominated as figurehead US plaintiffs in a big international lawsuit. We won a judgement of eight million dollars, none of which we saw, of course, or ever will. Such is the modern world.

I worked on for a couple of months and then stopped to leave for a mammoth month-long round-the-world tour, to launch *Past Tense*. Retirement was still on my mind and, if it happened for real anytime soon, I wanted to go out with a bang—revisiting all the stores and places that had been so kind to me in the past. I had gotten over the Lou Gehrig/John D. MacDonald superstition I mentioned in the essay on *Night School*, but there were still a couple of other issues on my mind.

The first was my frustration as a reader with favorite writers who seemed to have gotten bored or lazy or tired. As a young reader I felt betrayed and outraged. As an older reader, I supposed it must be inevitable. As I became a writer myself, I started to worry it would happen to me. I promised myself I would remain vigilant and quit as soon as I saw the first signs of running out of gas. I really didn't want to offer a substandard product. I didn't want my readers to feel as upset as I had. My instinct was to quit while I was ahead, and leave them wanting more.

The second issue was more general, but still related to how I had felt as a younger person. I hated that the older generation refused to get off the stage and leave space for the next generation. They stuck around forever, sucking up all the oxygen. I promised myself that I would never do that. An easy promise to make when you're twenty, but now I was sixty-four. Now I *was* the older generation. I had to decide whether to honor that ancient promise.

So the November 2018 world tour would be either a grand finale or just another milestone. I hadn't done anything as large and ambitious for eight years. Recent tours had been tight and compact. But I was up for it. I started in the US, focusing on the same stores and venues that had taken a chance on me for my first tour, twenty years before. Some of them had disappeared, of course—it had been a radical two decades in the book biz—so we filled the gaps with whatever quirky or interesting places we could find. Then I moved on to the UK—big venues in London, and I filled City Hall in Sheffield, my old college town, where as a student I saw all the big rock tours. Then came Australia, and finally New Zealand, the world capital of Reacher madness. Overall, the trip was a delight—a warm bath, with love and enthusiasm everywhere. Every author should be so lucky.

The flight back from Auckland to New York went via Singapore and Vancouver, at first basically following the International Date Line, so it was Monday, then Tuesday, then Monday again, and so on. Cathay Pacific was terrific—my first-class "room" was huge, with an actual queen-size bed, and free pajamas nicer than any I actually owned. I slept fourteen hours at one point. Door to door the trip was thirty-seven hours, and ten minutes after I got home, a journalist from the *London Sunday Times* showed up, an appointment I had forgotten about.

I got back to work the next day, and plugged away all winter. The story unspooled very nicely, I thought. Poor old Mr. (and Mrs.) Shevick were indeed in lots of trouble. Reacher helped them out, sometimes with spectacular savagery. I would write a set-up scene and think, *OK, what now? Oh, just kill them all*, I would decide. Was that waning imagination on my part, or a justified response to some seriously unpleasant villains? I wasn't sure.

I finished the book in April 2019, and was pleased with it. It was published that fall, and did well. It hit number one everywhere. It was well reviewed and seemed well thought of. Did it betray signs I was running out of gas? To be personally hypercritical, yes, I thought, possibly, in places, but I felt that no one else would interpret it that way. I don't think I let myself or my readers down. At least I sincerely hoped not.

Would it be the last book? It was the last in my current contract. Would I retire now? I suppose the only way to find out is to turn the page and see if there's another essay to follow.

A BETTER PLACE

A JACK REACHER STORY

Reacher ate lunch at a barbecue pit deep in the piney woods west of Birmingham, Alabama. After his meal he sat a spell and then waited with his thumb out where the parking lot met the road. The lot was beaten red dirt and the road was the same. All around were trees two hundred feet tall, as straight as chimneys, densely packed, turning the afternoon light dim and gloomy.

The very next customer to leave offered him a ride. The guy was a sawmill worker headed for the middle of nowhere. He said he would let Reacher out where the back road crossed the county road. He said his chances would be better there. Plenty of traffic. Well, some. Loggers, mostly. Whether they could pick up passengers depended on whether their insurance company allowed it. Some did, a lot didn't. But there were regular vehicles too. Pickups, mostly. Some cars. Now and then. Not many. All in all, he said, the wooded part of Alabama was very poor hitchhiking territory. The rest of the state wasn't much better. A lonely and dangerous venture, wherever you were, not to be undertaken lightly.

The guy's face was as green and gloomy as the afternoon light. Reacher wasn't sure if he was getting some kind of a redneck wind-up routine. Maybe he had been taken for a Yankee tourist. Maybe now he was supposed to hear banjos in his head. He had seen that movie. He liked the soundtrack. The action, not so much. Too long. The real-life running time should have been about eleven minutes. The first encounter was dispositive. The best way to win a fight was to understand exactly when it starts.

Reacher said, "You picked me up in less than a minute. That's about as good as it gets. Not poor territory at all."

The guy said, "I'm the exception that proves the rule."

"Or probes it. The Latin root means both."

"How could it?"

"Small vocabulary. Not many words. Not enough to go around. Some had to double up."

"That's crazy."

"I think yours is a very hospitable state. I got here yesterday. I haven't been lonely, and I certainly haven't felt in any kind of danger."

The guy didn't answer. Reacher looked out the window. Trees everywhere, red dirt, stacks of logs, tangled piles of thin branches and Y-shaped lumps where heavy boughs had met their trunks. The car slowed. There was a yellow crossroads sign, tilted over, riddled with shotgun pellets.

"This is it," the guy said. "North to the left and south to the right. I wish you the best of luck, sir. I finish work nine hours from now. If you're still here, I'll take you back to the barbecue. You can sleep in a hollow log and try again tomorrow."

The county road was as straight as a ruler but not as flat as a pancake. It rode up and down, over small hills and short dales, like the swells on an ocean. It was made of good blacktop and had a bright yellow center line that disappeared in the dips and came back like morse code on the next rounded peak, and the next, for miles. It was twice as wide as the dirt road from the barbecue and had cleared shoulders each twice as wide as the traffic lanes themselves. A firebreak, not just a solid county two-lane.

There was no traffic. No sound. The light was bright. The firebreak was about two hundred feet wide in total. Sunshine flooded in. Reacher walked out to the center line and held his face up to the light. There was a thin plume of smoke on the far horizon to the north. Something burning, maybe fifteen miles away. Or something just extinguished. There was nothing to the south except the yellow dots and dashes disappearing into the hazy distance.

No traffic. No sound.

No point just standing there.

Reacher walked south on the gritty shoulder, up the rises, down the dips, three of them, then four, and on the fifth he walked up the slope and saw a vehicle stopped dead about a quarter mile ahead of him, down in the next dip, previously hidden from sight. Facing south, on the same side of the road as him. It was a pickup truck, he thought, with what looked like a woman standing next to it. She was kicking it. Kicking the back wheel, maybe. She looked mad as hell about something.

Still no traffic. Still no sound, except muffled clangs and yelps from a quarter mile ahead. Which stopped after a minute. The woman stood still. Maybe she was tired. Maybe she was calling a tow truck. Was she getting reception? Reacher doubted it. Too far from anywhere. But he had no way of knowing. He didn't have a phone. He walked on. The truck looked small. Some kind of a junior model, maybe. Regular tires and a four-cylinder motor. The woman looked small, too. Pale red hair, almost-white shirt, worn blue jeans. Like a faded flag.

She saw him. She started toward him, one step, a flash of relief in her face, and then she stopped, disappointed. He was wearing a stained blue T-shirt, not a crisp item with *Speedy Auto Repair* embroidered above the pocket. He was empty-handed, not lugging giant tool bags crammed with useful hardware. Plus she was a small woman, and he was a huge man, and there was no traffic, and no sound.

Reacher stopped twenty feet away. Unthreatening. The woman stood her ground. She was about five-two. The red hair looked like the real thing. She still looked disappointed. Her truck had a flat tire. Rear wheel, passenger side. Within his range of automotive capabilities, which was limited.

"Need a hand?" he asked.

"I need a jack," she said.

"My first name."

"To change the tire."

"Happy to help."

"No," she said. "I need a jack to jack the truck up off the ground so I can get the wheel off the hub. You don't have a jack. I can see that from here. They don't fit in a pocket."

"Why would I have a jack? I have to say, I've been all over, and I never saw random pedestrians carrying car jacks just for the fun of it. It doesn't happen."

"Evidently."

"Isn't there one in the truck?"

"You think I haven't looked?"

"Everywhere?"

"Literally."

"May I approach?"

"Me?"

"The truck," Reacher said.

"Why? You think I didn't look properly?"

"I'm sure you did. There is no jack. I believe you. So we need a plan B."

"Such as what?"

"I don't know yet. It might involve trees."

"You're wasting my time."

"What's down the road?"

"Why?"

"It's where I'm headed. I'm about to keep on going. Believe me, I'm equally happy not to help."

"There's nothing much down the road."

"Got to be something."

"Literally the next thing is a hamburger shack about ten miles on."

"They got a phone?"

"Obviously."

"I'll call a tow truck for you."

"How will you get there?"

"Walk," he said.

"That would take forever."

"Two and a half hours," he said. "I like walking. Plenty of time for contemplation. Past events, and future plans."

"How would plan B involve trees?"

"Parts of trees, to be technical. First I have to find the right kind. You stay there. Anyone comes by, make them stop. They'll have a jack."

No traffic. No sound.

He crossed the cleared shoulder to where the forest restarted. In the gloomy margin was a straggling pile of thin branches of no commercial value, held down by the big Y-shaped lumps he had seen before. They weren't really logs in any salable sense. But they were as thick as logs.

He hefted one up and carried it back. He laid it down next to the truck. It was thick enough. It would do the job. He rotated it until the thickest stem of the Y was facing forward. Then he pulled it back six inches. Locked and loaded. He stepped back, satisfied.

He said, "Now you have to do something I'm guessing you won't want to."

"Like what?" she said.

"Lie down on your back."

"Your guess was correct."

"The plan is I raise up the back of the truck and you shove the wood under the side rail of the frame with your feet."

"You can deadlift a pickup truck?"

"No one can deadlift a pickup truck. I'm going to bounce it. You'll have to get the timing right. Safest way is to lie on your back and kick the wood under with your feet."

"It's called a crotch, I think. Where a big branch joins the trunk. You want me to kick the crotch."

"In a manner of speaking."

"Will it work?"

"Maybe."

She took her phone out of her pocket and stared at it, as if a signal might have magically appeared. Apparently it hadn't. She put the phone back in her pocket. She said, "OK, let's do it."

"Loosen the lugs first. It might be somewhat unstable. You don't want to be applying a whole lot of torque while it's resting on the wood."

She got to work with the tire iron. Four lugs only. A junior model. Regular tires and plain steel wheels. The spare was in a cradle under the rear end. She used the tire iron again and lowered the wheel on a chain. Reacher hauled it out. It was stained orange from back-road dirt. He placed it the right way around, handy for where they were going to need it.

The load bed was scratched and the tailgate was dented. The Alabama plate was bent and attached with one screw only. The rear bumper was ratty and not structural. There was a tow hitch welded to the frame. Lower than he would have liked, but nevertheless his best bet.

He said, "Get ready."

She sat down on the blacktop and put the flat of her feet against the wood, and then lay down on her back, with her knees up and her small hands pressed against the road for purchase, her neck bent and her head raised to watch the side of the truck. Reacher crouched a little and linked his hands and cupped them under the hitch. He tested the weight. The back of the truck came up on its suspension. He dropped it back down and it bounced an inch. He timed the sprung momentum and heaved upward again, and let it fall, and caught the bounce, and heaved it up some more, and again, and again, three inches, four, six, eight, ten, grunting and gasping, until the woman snapped her legs straight and pushed the wood neatly under the frame rail.

The flat tire was hanging two inches above the road. The woman stood up. She spun the lugs the rest of the way and wrestled the wheel off the hub. Reacher slung it in the load bed. He lifted the spare and held it on the hub. The woman spun the lugs tight. Reacher took the iron and tightened them more, until they squealed.

Job done.

Almost.

The woman asked, "How do we get the wood out again?"

Reacher clapped the dirt off his hands and said, "I'll lift the side an inch and you haul it out."

"You said no one could do that."

"All we need is an inch. I had a big lunch."

He squatted down again, with his hands hooked under the frame rail and his chest against the side of the load bed. He took a breath and lifted the weight and the woman said, "It's out," and he dropped the truck back down.

He breathed out. The new tire looked good, except it was orange with dirt. He said, "I'll go put the wood back in the pile. We shouldn't leave trash in the firebreak." He hefted it up and walked back the way he had brought it. He dropped it on the pile.

He turned back and saw the woman drive away without him.

Two and a half hours later he made it to the hamburger shack. He had been passed by two log haulers, two pickup trucks, and an old beat-up Cadillac convertible. None of them had even slowed down to take a look at him. They had all barreled past in howls of air and grit. Maybe the gloomy sawmill guy was right after all. Not prime hitchhiking territory.

The hamburger shack was a swaybacked wooden affair that could have been built out of boards milled from the trees evidently removed to make the parking lot. There were two windows and a door in the front wall, and a metal kitchen chimney poking up through the roof, with a greasy haze of heat shimmering out of it. The beat-up Cadillac that had passed him so indifferently was parked in the lot alongside two full-fat pickup trucks and two Harley-Davidson motorcycles.

Reacher had eaten a big lunch, but he was hungry again, due to his exertions. He went in the door and stood for a moment. The interior was dim. There was a griddle in back, and a counter, and ten tables, five on one side of the room and five on the other. The side to Reacher's right was empty, and the side to his left was occupied by five guys, two of them pacing, three of them sitting. All five of them were agitated. Reacher had been a military cop for a good long spell and he knew how to read collective group emotions. An important professional skill, both for the units he led, and for the units he busted.

His assessment was these guys all knew each other well, either through some kind of employment, or recreation, or crime. Whichever it was, their little world was under attack. Something bad had happened. Not minutes ago, but hours ago. They were over the immediate shock. Their agitation came from not knowing what to do about it. They had hustled over for an emergency meeting. Five vehicles, five guys. They had talked, but they had reached no conclusions.

Not my circus, not my monkeys, Reacher thought. He stepped up to the counter and ordered a cheeseburger, no fries, onion rings on the side. Plus coffee. "Don't got none," the cook said. "Soda pop only." Reacher chose Coke. The next best thing.

He waited alone at a table on the right side of the room. The five guys were talking. Reacher heard the name Caleb mentioned, over and over. He was one of them, but he wasn't there. That was the source of their agitation. Reacher narrowed down his initial theory. They were a skanky bunch. Probably unemployable, so they didn't know each other from work. They didn't look like hobby types either, so recreation was also off the table. Which left crime. Maybe Caleb was the sixth musketeer, and maybe he had been busted, and maybe he was busy ratting them out, right at that moment. Criminal enterprises falling apart usually produced agitation among the participants.

Then one of the pacing guys turned and paced the other way, whereby his gaze passed over Reacher's patient form, which produced a double take. The Cadillac driver, Reacher assumed. The guy said, "I saw this mofo on the road down here. He was hitching rides. Biggest damn mofo I saw all year."

The other four turned to look at Reacher. One of the sitting-down guys said, "He was walking south? Away from Caleb's?"

"He sure was."

The guy got up out of his chair. He took two steps toward Reacher. He said, "Hello, stranger. You want to tell us what you're doing here?"

The best way to win a fight was to understand exactly when it starts. Which was right then, obviously. Reacher said nothing. The guy said, "I'm talking to you. You going to answer me?"

Reacher looked at him, right in the eye. Said nothing.

The guy said, "Someone just burned Caleb's trailer. With him in it."

A thin plume of smoke on the far horizon to the north.

"Then they stole his momma's truck. I think it was you."

"You think?" Reacher said. "Is that a new experience? Clearly you're not very good at it yet. If I stole Caleb's momma's truck, why would I be hitching rides?"

"You better watch your mouth, pal."

Reacher sat still.

The guy stepped a pace closer.

He said, "You better start talking, boy."

Reacher said, "It isn't really working, is it?"

"What ain't?"

"This is you being scary, right? Ineffective so far, I'm afraid. Because I'm not. Afraid, that is. Not of you."

"Stand up and come here and say that to my face."

Reacher stood up. He moved his table aside. He stepped up close to the guy. He spread his fingers and patted the air, palms out, a *whoa* gesture, as if to say *calm down*, conciliating, placating. But really to get his hands up to neck height unnoticed and to make a nice L shape between his left thumb and his left index finger.

He said, "The thing is," and stabbed the L shape into the guy's throat and bunched his right hand into a fist and hit the guy in the left eye, hard enough to break bones. The guy went down like a shot horse. Just a dusty thump on the floorboards. One and done. No further participation. Not like in the movies.

There was silence for a second. Then another guy piled in. Reacher kicked him in the nuts as soon as he was within range and then kicked him behind the knees, which dumped him on the floor. The Cadillac driver came next, but didn't survive a straight right to the solar plexus and a perfect uppercut to the jaw, which damn near took his head off. Numbers four and five came in together, one of them armed with a chair. Reacher took it from him and used it to break the other guy's arm before swinging it viciously the other way and clotheslining the first guy in the neck.

Five up, five down. Five seconds. Blows delivered, eight. Blows received, zero. A perfect game.

The cook called out, "Your cheeseburger is ready."

Reacher called back, "Do you know these guys?"

"I've seen them time to time. I'd like to see them less. Your meal is on the house tonight."

Reacher took all the cash he found in the five guys' pockets, plus the Cadillac driver's keys. He eased himself into the sagging seat and started the motor. It caught with a loud wet burble. The gear selector was on the steering column. He slid it into drive and moved away. He was a poor driver but it was an easy car. Everything was power assisted. It was a one-finger, one-toe proposition, built for lazy wafting, riding like a cloud. The road was dead straight. No complications. He drove for hours, deep into the night, until he saw a sign promising a motel ten miles ahead. Which was the first he had seen for a couple of hundred miles. Which meant maybe the next would be another couple hundred. Too long. Too late. Too tired. Better to take the immediate ten-mile option.

He pulled off the road and followed a dirt driveway through trees as high as buildings to a clearing containing a cookie-cutter motel, similar to a thousand he had patronized before, this one imaginatively named *Motel Pine*, which was written on a lit sign at the top of a pole disguised as a pine tree. It was plumper than the real thing. It could have been a Christmas tree, and probably was, one month a year.

Reacher brought the floating car to a wobbling stop at the motel office. He paid for a room with Caleb's friends' money and got back in the car. He drove down the row, past the room he had been given. He figured there would be a maintenance alley behind the building. He was pretty sure the Cadillac's owner wouldn't be calling the cops anytime soon, but even so, he was in a stolen vehicle with no license, insurance, or registration. Better to park out of sight and dump it in the morning. He made the 180 turn.

Someone else had the same idea. The Cadillac's yellow headlight beams lit up a pickup truck parked in the alley. It was small. Some kind of a junior model, maybe. A four-cylinder engine. Plain steel wheels. Regular tires, one of them stained orange.

It had a Florida plate now. Two screws. But it was the same truck. Same dents, same scratches. Flat tire in the load bed. Same tow hitch. Reacher knew it well.

He parked the Cadillac right behind it.

Which room was she in? He walked around to the front. Twelve rooms. Eight with open curtains, hence seven unoccupied, plus his. He hadn't been in it yet. There were three with curtains closed and cars outside. There was one with curtains closed and no car outside. Because it was in back. Her room.

He knocked at her door and stepped back to watch the window. Sure enough, the curtain pinched into a small oval hole, and he saw the glint of an eye. The door opened on the chain.

She said, "Who are you, exactly?"

"The same as you," Reacher said. "I drove all night and decided to take a break."

"And knocked on this door randomly?"

"I was in a stolen car, too. I parked in the alley."

"That's my truck."

"No, it isn't. You're a smart, organized, practical, capable person. No way would your car be missing a jack."

She didn't answer.

"Word in the county is a guy named Caleb has a momma who got her truck stolen. She sounds like a person who might not run a monthly checklist. I bet it's a long time since she got her oil changed. Or checked her tire treads for nails."

The woman said nothing.

"I met five of Caleb's friends. Not the finest specimens I ever encountered."

No answer.

"Was Caleb as bad as them?"

"I don't know anyone called Caleb."

"Why didn't you give me a ride? I bet normally you're a kind and thoughtful person. But you were stressed. Why steal a Florida plate? You're running and hiding."

"Are you a cop?"

"I was, once upon a time, in the military. Now I'm just a regular civilian."

She was quiet for a long moment. Making up her mind. She unlatched the chain.

"Come in," she said.

Her room was standard in every way. She had no bags. Running and hiding, spur of the moment.

"Who was Caleb?" Reacher asked.

"He cooked meth. My brother owed him money. Couldn't pay. Caleb had him beaten up. Probably by the five you met. They went too far. He died from his injuries."

"I'm sorry. That's bad. I know how you feel."

"Do you?"

"My brother was murdered too. I told you, we're the same."

"What did you do about it?"

"I found them, shot some of them, drowned one of them, and burned the rest in a fire."

She was quiet again.

She asked, "What should I do now?"

Reacher gave her the Cadillac key.

"Leave the truck here. Use the Cadillac to get to a city or a town. No one is looking for it yet. Park it on a back street with the key in. Take a bus or a train. You'll be OK. The cops aren't interested. Meth labs burn all the time. It's a NHI case."

"What's NHI?"

"No humans involved. The cops don't care. They won't bust a gut. They'll figure the fire left the world a better place."

She looked at the Cadillac key. "How will you get out of here?"

"I'll walk," Reacher said. "I like walking. Plenty of time for contemplation. Past events, and future plans."

AFTERWORD
A NOTE FROM THE PUBLISHER

With no trace of flamboyance, Lee Child can dominate a room with a soft voice and inclusive demeanor, taking in everyone—while everyone has the sense that he is speaking directly to them. It may not be possible to define this precisely, but the word charisma is as close as I can come when thinking of Lee, as the multitudes who have met him, or even seen him, will surely agree.

It may seem to be counterintuitive, but this elegant charm permeates his books. At first blush, the Jack Reacher series appears to be a continuum of violent

AFTERWORD

episodes, paused from time to time as he decides whether to become involved, how serious the obstacles might be, and the consequences of his behavior to those with whom he interacts.

Boiled down to a cliché, Reacher is a vigilante. Though he knows and believes in the law, he is willing to ignore it in the pursuit of justice. Innocent people in desperate circumstances are not in a position to parse the nuances of the law, nor are these nuances the first thing that crosses Reacher's mind. He encounters (or seeks) a situation in which he knows he can help and just forges ahead and does it. Not a lot of equivocating, no weighing of what-ifs, no checking his watch to be sure he has time to handle the situation. If someone—anyone—is in trouble, Reacher will step in and balance the odds.

As I have written previously, Reacher's character reflects the chivalrous knight errant of medieval lore, as opposed to the au courant anti-hero tormented by addiction and haunted by past misbehavior.

Lee Child is Jack Reacher. No, not physically. Lee is not 6'5" (well, almost) but Reacher might outweigh him by a hundred pounds, and Lee, like most of us, is unlikely to look for trouble. But the egalitarian view

AFTERWORD

of the world (to borrow Michael Connelly's maxim, "everybody counts or nobody counts") permeates the philosophy of both the author and his creation.

This sensibility endeared both Lee and Reacher to me many years ago, first when I read *Killing Floor* and *Die Trying*, and then when Lee started doing readings and attending parties at my bookshop, The Mysterious Bookshop in New York City. He was relentlessly gracious to everyone and I was among the fans who found being in his company an unmitigated pleasure. As years passed, we became friends.

Because of the friendship, and an absurdly inviolable devotion to the Reacher novels, I decided that I would like to do something special for them and asked Lee how he felt about The Mysterious Bookshop reissuing the entire series in elegant, limited editions. They were to be uniformly bound in marbled boards, leather spines stamped in gold, on fine paper. Each volume would be limited to no more than one hundred copies, numbered, and signed by him, as well as twenty-six lettered copies for presentation, promotion, and sale.

And here came the tricky question: Would he be willing to write a new foreword to each book,

AFTERWORD

describing the genesis of the story, where he was—both physically and emotionally—and anything else that seemed germane to placing each particular title in the context of the entire series. Lee said he liked the idea and would be happy to do it. The only remaining question was in what color would he like them bound, and we settled on a dark green, with the lettered copies bound in black.

I wasn't quite sure what to expect when the first foreword arrived on my computer. Over the years, I have asked numerous authors for introductions to books or stories and many have been excellent, thoughtful, and stylish. Others were, evidently, dashed off, resulting in short, superficial pieces essentially fulfilling an assignment but nothing more.

The prospect of Lee writing something pedestrian was neither an expectation nor a fear. That is not what he does. But I was concerned that he might just deliver a page or two that merely skimmed the surface and did not sufficiently provide enough new material to satisfy or excite the reader. As the first reader, I was satisfied, excited, *and* relieved. I never worried again.

AFTERWORD

As you will have noticed by now, this being an afterword to a book that you have read, Lee brings the same effortless style to his nonfiction writing as he does to his novels and stories. It would be easy to produce straightforward reportage to pieces of this sort. You know: "Just the facts, ma'am." But, no, reading even a line about the date or the locale goes down as smoothly as a heartbreak song from the blues guitar of John Littlejohn.

Having loved all these mini-essays that introduce the next Jack Reacher adventure, it made sense to see them collected in book form. Until now, these original and important looks behind the curtain on the construction of Lee's worldwide bestsellers had been seen by only one hundred twenty-six lucky readers. It was time to share them with everybody.

This book is the result.

—Otto Penzler
New York, February 2025